Only a Priest

M.O.Chamberlain

ONLY A PRIEST

2nd Edition

ISBN: 978-0-473-62016-5 Paperback
978-0-473-62017-2 Kindle

www.mochamberlain.com

DEDICATION

To all good priests still holding the line.

ACKNOWLEDGMENTS

I would like to acknowledge all the good priests, living and dead, who inspired this book, especially those who generously gave of their time to share with me their lives in the vocation. I would like to thank those who have been or are currently involved in the ministry of exorcism and shared their experiences with me. I would also like to acknowledge the Columban Missionary Society, in particular, a Columban priest, a good friend of mine, whose life story forms, in large measure, though not entirely, the material for the character of Father Peter Gilbert. Finally, I would like to thank Dr Lyn Wytenbroeck for her invaluable editorial assistance.

Who would want to be a priest
When they call for one to fight the Beast

Chapter One

He was old and infirm and had to pull over often to rest. His car was old as well and the battered small suitcase from which he took the sandwiches he had made for the journey was hardly new. His thermos was though. A gift from his nephew. He offered a cup of the hot brew of tea he had prepared early that morning to the hitch-hiker.

The young man was restless. This was the second time the old fellah had stopped for a cup of tea. He considered trying for another ride but there was little traffic on the road and the old fellah's kai was good: ham sandwiches with just the right amount of mustard between thick slices of homemade bread. The food put him in the mood to talk. "Just been released from prison. On my way home."

The old man kept eating his sandwich and sipping his tea. He was not a big talker.

"Yeah," said the young man, "got eight months for drunk driving. It was number seven though. They warned me. But I couldn't help myself back then."

This old fellah had a twinkle in his eye and a half smile, like he had some happy secret. The young man watched him pause to consider what he had said.

"Yeah, I'm different now, eh. Done some of them courses in prison. Got me a programme. No more drinking, eh. I'm an alcoholic, that's for sure."

The old man looked him in the eye.

He wasn't an easy read this old fellah. He didn't say much and when he looked him in the eye the young man felt he was seeing things, like one of those old kaumatua at the marae knowing things about him without being told.

"Yeah, one drink is one too many. Nothing's so bad that drinking won't make it worse." The young man had the recovering alcoholic's dictums off by heart.

The old fellah just nodded. He wasn't giving much away. Not an easy read. Fellahs in prison, they were easy to read. The angry ones, they had that cold look. You stayed away from them 'cause they loved to fight. The friendly ones, they were usually weak, wanting a friend. And the psychos, the cruel ones, you needed to know when they were having a bad day. Old fellahs in prison were usually dumb buggers who liked three squares and a bed at night and couldn't make a life for themselves on the outside.

"What about you?"

The old man smiled. "My name's Peter."

"Hemi," said the young man, extending his hand.

"I've been retired but now I've got a job."

"Oh, yeah. Sweet."

The old man screwed the lid back on his Thermos and folded up the greaseproof paper he had wrapped the sandwiches in. Hemi sensed this old fellah had mana, lots of it, there was something important about him, but he couldn't put his finger on it.

"What kind of a job?"

The old man laughed. He liked that about Maori people. It was all out there. No secrets. "Well," he said, "a friend of mine needs some help."

"Oh yeah," said Hemi, "sort of thing an old fellah can do, eh?"

"You could say that."

"I thought an old fellah like you'd be living the good life. Catching fish and stuff like that."

"Retirement's overrated."

"So, what kind of job is it?"

The old man considered this question as though it was difficult to answer. "This friend of mine is having trouble with an old enemy, and he wants me up there to help sort him out."

Hemi's head shot up at this. "Ho, man. Far out. No disrespect, but you seem a bit old to be someone's back-up."

The old man laughed and leaned on his waking stick to stand up and walk around to the driver's door of his car. He grabbed the steering wheel and pulled himself in.

Hemi climbed in and watched him take off his fedora hat, put his sunglasses on and his seatbelt and then put the gear stick into neutral. He was so old and slow, like one of those old lags who come into prison for the first time, being friendly with everyone. They learned pretty quick. This fellah shouldn't have picked him up. An old fellah like him picking up a hitch-hiker. No good. Some fellahs would take him for everything he had 'cause it would be so easy. Not him, though. He wasn't up for that, not anymore. This old fellah was like his koro, someone you looked after.

They headed out onto the road and the old man adjusted the car's sun visor. Traffic was building and other cars were speeding past. "So, this old enemy, how yous gunna deal to him?" asked Hemi, the idea having occurred to him that maybe he and his mates could help this old fellah and his friend.

"Carefully," replied the old man.

"No disrespect, but you seem a bit old."

"Too old for what?"

"Well, fighting a mate's enemy."

"More than one way to fight."

Hemi thought about this for a while. "Okay, I get you. My old koro is always on about that, 'Hemi, using your fists is for stupid people.' Always saying stuff like that. My whanau they like to fight, eh. But not my koro. Nah, he's done with that. Goes to church and all that."

"Good for him."

"Yeah, he's better for it, eh." Hemi chuckled.

"Something funny?"

"No. No. Just thinking of this rap I wrote for my koro. You want to hear it?"

The old man nodded and Hemi pulled a piece of paper from his pocket.

"When you're old and slow.
Don't have to go toe to toe.
Just stay in the light.
Keep it shining bright
And you'll be alright."

"Not bad," said the old man.

"You a church fellah, too, eh?"

"Yeah, you could say that."

"Me, I'm no church fellah, but I'm trying to be good, eh. Be good and good things happen."

The old man nodded and Hemi could see he was distracted by something and stopped talking.

There was a shift in the balance of things when the old man's car crossed the county line and he could feel it: a weakening and a strengthening. Whether it was his imagination only or something prompting it, he could never be sure. He glanced across at his passenger and wondered how much he understood about wairua. "This enemy of mine knows I'm coming and his mates know, too."

"You worried?" asked Hemi.

"No. I have mates, too."

The temperature gauge on the old Ford was signalling time for a rest and the old man stopped at the top of the Mangamukas for another cup of tea from a viewpoint that enabled them to see for miles to the north. They had been motoring through hilly country, but now, like a bunched-up carpet suddenly pulled free, they could see the land northwards opening up into a flat coastal plain, battered by wild seas to the west and lapped by quieter waters to the east. The old man pressed down the radiator cap and turned it. Steam hissed out and he left it.

Hemi had been walking around the car, taking in all its features. "This is one of those vintages, eh? Be worth a bit. Hard case it still goes, eh?"

The old man nodded and they sat together on the running board of the Ford and shared the last of the tea in the Thermos. It was late afternoon and there was a chill in the air. The long, warm days of summer were still with them, but a southerly was coming up from the Antarctic.

Hemi's grandparents' farm was only a few more miles further down the road and he was in good spirits. "I usually go straight to town when I come back. Score some gear and get wasted. Not this time. Going to my koro's. Help him on his farm. My nan'll be good for a feed if you want to stop."

The old man smiled. "Thank you, but I need to get to where I'm going."

"So, this enemy, he knows you're coming, eh?"

"Oh, he knows alright."

"Pretty cunning."

The old man nodded and gave Hemi a look he rightly read as a cue to stop talking. The old fellah looked very tired and it took a big effort to get onto his feet. Hemi moved in to support him but was nudged away. "I'm alright," said the old man sternly.

He was a proud old bugger, hated being old. Hemi could see that and could see he was also too tired to be bothered talking anymore. He lapsed into silence and left him to concentrate on his driving.

The silence was awkward and the old man regretted not making more of an effort with the young man. Wanting to give him something, he broke the silence and spoke to him. "Last time I met up with this enemy he threw me across the room. Broke my shoulder and my leg. I came at him too hard and too long. Made some bad moves. I learned from that."

"Whoa," said Hemi, narrowing his eyes, studying the old man, unsure of what to make of him now, wondering if he was in his right mind. "How old is this fellah?"

"He's been around a long, long time. I wouldn't call him old. Ancient's a better word. In fact, he's been around since before time began."

Hemi paused to consider this. "That don't make sense."

"'Been around for a long, long years, Stole million man's soul an faith.'"

Hemi was still frowning.

"Rolling Stones. Sympathy for the Devil," said the old man.

The light was not coming on for Hemi and he was pleased they were coming up to where he wanted to be dropped off. There were fellahs in prison who talked about the devil and the smart play was to steer well clear of them.

"You can drop me off just up here," said Hemi.

"I can take you to your grandfather's place."

"That's alright."

"No trouble," said the old man and he turned left onto a road that led to the marae where Hemi's grandfather lived in a house out the back.

The old man recognised the house and wondered if the people living there would still remember him. It had been years. If the kaumatua who shuffled out to greet his mokopuna did remember, he gave no sign of it. He was more focussed on solemnly shaking his grandson's hand and giving him a hongi. But then he turned to the car and went around to the driver's side and beamed when he was sure it was who he thought it was. "Same car, same man," he laughed. "Tena koe, old friend."

The old man climbed out and hongi'ed.

"Good to see you, Father Gilbert," said the kaumatua

and the priest laughed.

"You haven't forgotten?"

"No, never forget a good fellah," he said and turned to his grandson. "This fellah been any trouble?"

"No, he's been keeping me company. Riding shotgun. There to defend me if there was trouble."

"Ah, that's him alright." He nodded approval to Hemi, still at odds with what he had just learned, and pointed to the house. "Tell your grandmother to put the kettle on."

The priest held up his hand. "Thank you, Manu, but I have to be going. Another time."

Hemi and his grandfather stood to watch the old Ford bumping its way along the rutted road out of the marae. "That fellah a priest?" asked Hemi.

His grandfather did not answer. He was lost in his own thoughts, a far-off look in his eyes. Eventually, he came back to his grandson and smiled at him. "When they let you out?"

"This morning."

They walked back to the house in silence and Hemi's grandmother, waiting on the front porch for them, could not hold back another moment and rushed down to hug her mokopuna.

"That was Father Gilbert," said her husband.

And Hemi watched as his grandmother faltered, then paused and was lost in her own thoughts, too, as she looked down the road to where the priest had gone.

"Fifteen years since that priest was last here," said Hemi's grandfather.

"I don't remember him," said Hemi.

His grandmother laughed. "You were a young fellah

running around causing trouble as usual. Only here a few weeks. Came up from Auckland to give Father Murphy a break."

"Fifteen years. Almost to the day, last month," said Manu, coming back to them from a daydream. "Never forget that man."

"Why not?" asked Hemi.

Both grandparents seem to ignore this question and Hemi knew better than to push too hard, but that night, while he was doing the dishes with his grandmother, she answered him. "We'd had an unveiling and the drinking had gone on a bit long for my liking. I told them they needed to go home. Your uncle was one of them. It was the unveiling for his wife. She'd died of cancer, and he could never get his act together after she passed. Was drunk that night, like most nights but he insisted on driving. They tried to wrestle the keys off him, but he was too strong.

"Anyway, he took off like a bat out of hell, out of the marae, down the road and straight out onto the main road, right into the path of a truck. Everyone heard the crash and we all rushed down, and there he was trapped in his car. I knew he wasn't going to make it. There was just no way. Blood everywhere. He was a mess. Your grandfather called the ambulance and the fire brigade to cut him out. And I called the priest.

"It was two in the morning. I knew the priest would be in bed and I'd probably just get an answer phone but I called. The phone went on ringing and ringing, but no answerphone message so I held on. Must have been a few minutes and I was thinking it was a waste of time when this Father Gilbert came on the line. I told him what had happened and he said he'd be there as soon as he could.

"Twenty minutes later that Ford of his came belting down the road. He already had his stole around his neck and came hurrying over with his prayer book in his hand. He grabbed hold of our Kenny's hand and told him he was there to pray for him. Kenny's hand was covered in blood but that old priest he took it gently in his and . . ." She stopped and closed her eyes, her face contorted, tears spilling down her face.

"The blood was running down Kenny's arm," continued Manu, putting his arm around his wife. "It was running onto the priest's jacket soaking it through. Father Gilbert made a sign of the cross on Kenny's forehead and Kenny looked into that priest's eyes and told him he didn't want to die. He was afraid. And old Father Gilbert he told him there was nothing to be afraid of. He put his rosary beads around Kenny's neck and he told Kenny he was there to hear his confession and Kenny nodded.

"I'll never forget that. Kenny nodded. My young fellah who hated church and had been angry with God for the death of his wife, he agreed to have this priest hear his confession. I never worked that one out. But this priest he had this strong manner and it was like I'm here to hear your confession and that's the way it's going to be.

"So we stepped back and left them to it. The Fire Brigade was there by then and they wanted the priest out of the way so they could cut Kenny out, but we told them, no let the priest finish and I'm glad we did. Kenny died while the priest was giving him absolution and he seemed peaceful. That same priest was there all through the tangi and did the funeral Mass so we got to know him real well. A good priest that one. And you getting a ride with him, that's big, boy, that's big."

Chapter Two

Father Gilbert arrived at the presbytery as the young parish priest he had come to help was sitting down to his evening meal. He knocked at the back door and waited. No one came which Father Gilbert found odd as he was sure he had heard noises from inside. He knocked again. The same silence followed and, not wanting to waste any more time on politeness, he went straight on in and found the parish priest in the dining room, his knife and fork poised above his plate.

"Father Ward?"

"Father Gilbert. I wasn't expecting you until tomorrow. The bishop said you were staying the night in Whangarei."

"His plan not mine," said Father Gilbert. "Did you not hear me knock?"

Father Ward smiled self-consciously. "The parishioners know I'm not to be disturbed at this time of the night."

Father Gilbert nodded thoughtfully.

"I'll help you bring in your things," said Father Ward, taking a napkin from his lap and placing it carefully on the table. He was impeccably dressed, his brown patent leather shoes shining.

"This is all," said Father Gilbert, indicating the small

case he'd set beside his leg. His shoes were scuffed and worn, and his suit had not been pressed in a long time. Father Ward escorted his guest to a room at the end of the house and left him to settle in. The old priest was not talkative.

From the kitchen, Father Ward listened to the sound of drawers being opened and shut and then there was silence. He wondered if the old priest was taking a rest. He had heard stories about Father Gilbert. Cryptic and enigmatic, a checkered history, intimidating, blunt and to the point. The reality of what he had set in motion weighed on him as he quickly finished his meal. Already there was a tension in the house. The silence. Wondering what to expect. His privacy gone. He sighed and put his plate and cutlery in the dishwasher.

The parish was Father Ward's first appointment as parish priest. It was a sole charge parish, and, until recently, Father Ward had handled the assignment well. But that was before the trouble with the Alexander boy.

"Don't worry about dinner for me," said Father Gilbert, suddenly there in the kitchen, filling the doorway, interrupting Father Ward reading the instructions on a packet of rice risotto. "I brought some homemade bread and luncheon sausage. Do you have butter and sauce?"

Father Ward nodded, replaced the packet in his pantry and skipped to the fridge.

"What's been happening since last we talked?"

Father Ward turned from where he stood inspecting the contents of his fridge. He had been told Father Gilbert was not a man for small talk and here it was. "Oh, yes," he said, taking sauce and butter to the kitchen table, "Uum. Well, he hasn't turned up for Mass since I spoke with his mother about you coming."

"He was coming to Mass?" asked Father Gilbert, surprised.

"Yes, he'd turn up on occasion and stand in the foyer. I formed the impression he was mocking me. It's what forced my hand."

"So you mentioned to the family you were contacting the bishop about an exorcist?"

"I did."

"Okay, well that's probably why he's lying low."

"Really?"

"If, as you believe, there's a demonic presence we need to be somewhat more prudent in our approach. For our wrestling is not against flesh and blood; but against principalities and powers, against the rulers of the world of this darkness, against the spirits of wickedness in the high places."

Father Ward recognised the quote. "I'm sorry," he said.

"Don't apologise, Father, I won't bore you with all the mistakes I've made. Tell me again, what made you contact the bishop?"

"Well, I went out there one day on a visitation. The mother asked me to. She had the idea her son was possessed and wanted me to pray for him. They're a very religious family. Mrs Alexander leads a rosary group and is very devout. Perhaps a little too devout."

"Too devout?"

"Well, I mean Mrs Alexander is always giving out holy pictures and scapulas after Mass and recommending some devotion or other. There are holy pictures in every room of the house, even a couple of statues. Very conservative Catholics, actually. She and her husband both have reservations about the new rite of the Mass and they often go down the line to attend Mass in Latin whenever it's available. Always watching out for anything she regards as sacrilegious or blasphemous. Someone receiving Holy Communion without due reverence, me giving communion to someone who hasn't received the sacrament, that sort of thing.

"I was somewhat skeptical about her version of what was happening with her son. On the one occasion I've seen him he did seem angry and withdrawn but nothing I saw as untoward. Just a typical teenager. He's about seventeen as I mentioned in my letter to the bishop. I also thought he was possibly rebelling against all the religiosity in the home. But not any longer." Father Ward sighed. The burden of what he had to share was not something he wanted to rush into. "Can I make you a cup of tea?" he asked.

"No. What happened to change your mind?"

"That day I went to visit, I had the idea I'd pray for the boy and bless him with holy water." Father Ward paused to shake his head. "That was a mistake. The boy was very restless while I was praying and when I brought out the holy water his whole demeanour changed. Very menacing, aggressive looking. Then, when I took out my crucifix, well, that's when things got out of control. He stood up from the kitchen table and tipped it over; and when his father, poor man, tried to restrain him, he seemed to just pick him up and toss him aside. And then he came at me. I'd put the crucifix away by then. Not wanting to agitate him any further. But it made no difference." Father Ward pursed his lips and raised his eyebrows. “Made no difference at all.”

“He came at you?”

“Yes.” Father Ward folded his arms.

“And?”

“Well, that was it really. I left, came home.”

“What did you do when he came for you?”

Father Ward took a big breath. “I um, I . . . I got out of there as quickly as I could.”

“You ran?”

“More or less,” said Father Ward, reluctantly. And then assertively, “Yes, I ran.”

Father Gilbert said nothing and Father Ward, blushing red, felt the need to explain. “He was speaking Latin, in a deep voice. A sinister voice. Not like the boy’s voice at all. Very unnerving. It frightened me.”

“Understandable,” said Father Gilbert, “but never run. Stand your ground in the name of Jesus. Anyway, more of that later.”

Father Ward smiled wryly. “The whole thing was a mistake. Imprudent. Very imprudent.”

“No,” said Father Gilbert. “You weren’t to know. And from what you’ve said there seems good grounds for believing in a possible possession and that’s a good thing. Under the new rite of exorcism, we’re not supposed to proceed unless we know it’s the devil. Of course, you don’t really know it’s the devil until you do proceed. As matters stand, what you described in your letter has prompted the bishop to send me without the usual step of involving a psychiatrist.”

“Psychiatrist?”

“Most of what people report as possession is usually

a mental issue."

"I did mention the family had been to the local psychological services."

"Yes, that helped too. Have you mentioned what happened to anyone in the parish?"

"No, no, no," said Father Ward, shaking his head vigorously. "Not something we talk about these days, is it? I mean the devil, hell, possession. Who mentions those things these days?" He failed to add that he had, once, to his regret.

"Not in this country," Father Gilbert agreed. "Different in some of the missionary countries I've worked in. Countries where they're not long out of paganism. Two thousand years of Christianity have sealed our borders, so to speak."

"The devil was hardly spoken of in the seminary," said Father Ward.

"Yes, I know what you mean. Any professor who did would be struggling for a contemporary reading list. Not one book written on Satan by any theologian in the whole of the twentieth century."

"Goodness," said Father Ward, intrigued.

"Yes," said Father Gilbert nodding slowly. "And it's when we think Satan no longer exists, he's at his most powerful. Just imagine if policemen in this country believed there were no more burglars and dismissed anyone claiming to have been burgled as a looney. Burglars would have a field day."

"Yes, well," said Father Ward looking at his watch. "I'll leave you to make those sandwiches. Sauce, butter, bread board," he said, indicating what he'd put on the table and heading for the lounge. "It's time for the news."

Father Gilbert carved off door stopping pieces of bread and, glancing up at the cross Father Ward had set above the door frame, smiled. The kitchen was meticulously tidy, surfaces shone and nothing was out of place. He was something of a dandy this young priest but he seemed to know the importance of the cross.

With three sandwiches stacked on a plate, he went into the lounge. When he was finished eating, he rubbed his hands and brushed the crumbs from his knees onto the floor. Father Ward's eyes narrowed, unnoticed by Father Gilbert. With the meal finished, it was time to become acquainted with the priest he was going to work with. "So," he said, above the sound of the newscaster, "what's your story?"

"Ah, sorry," said Father Ward, glancing from the television to Father Gilbert and back to the television.

"What's your story? Why are you a priest?"

Father Ward picked up the television remote and pressed mute.

"Waste of time watching that rubbish," said Father Gilbert, waving dismissively at the television, "we've got better things to do with our time. I'll have that cup of tea now if you're still offering. You did well taking holy water and a cross. Right thing to do."

"Thank you," said Father Ward and, taking Father Gilbert's lead, decided he would get straight to the point as well, "I had the idea we could go out there early next week."

"No," said Father Gilbert, "that wouldn't do. He's lying low at the moment. So, we'll leave things be. Never any hurry in these matters. From what you've told me we might be dealing with an exhibitionist who enjoys causing trouble. He'll be back. Eventually. Won't be able to resist.

And what better place than a church to have fun? Perfect place to show off with impunity. Patience and tolerance is what he'll be expecting."

Father Ward was frowning.

"Always tempting to hurry these things. The last one I tried to hurry landed me in the hospital. That's when they retired me. Now what time's Mass tomorrow morning?"

"We don't have Mass on Tuesdays."

"Really?"

"Mass is on Wednesdays, Fridays and Sundays."

Father Ward did not wait for Father Gilbert's response to this. He turned off the television and left to make a cup of tea. He was clearly irritated but resigned himself to the inevitable. Whether he liked it or not, he needed this old priest's help, blunt and seemingly insensitive though he obviously was. Why was he a priest? Father Gilbert's unanswered question came back at him. Why was he a priest? That was a big one. Lately, with all the trouble he'd been having, he'd been asking himself the same question. In fact, when he thought back on all he had put up with since he had arrived at this parish a more appropriate question would have been: why was he *still* a priest?

Mrs Gaffney, the housekeeper, had baked some scones and while he waited for the tea to draw Father Ward buttered some and spooned some plum jam into a small glass dish. Loading everything onto a tray, he went into his guest who had pushed back the La-Z-Boy recliner into a horizontal position and was sound asleep. Slack jawed and snoring gently, Father Gilbert was pale with fatigue and seemed very old. Not wishing to disturb him, Father Ward sat in silence sipping his tea, at ease for the first time since his guest had arrived. He took another bite of scone and made a mental note to let Mrs Gaffney know he was catching the slightest hint of baking soda in her normally blemish-free soft clouds of gluten. He applied more jam to hide the bitter taste.

Chapter Three

Father Ward remembered clearly the day he had first arrived in the parish after a long drive up from Auckland in the new vehicle his family had given him on the day of his ordination. His first assignment as a parish priest. He arrived towards the end of February, two years previously. The presbytery had been closed up for over a week and he was overcome by the stifling heat inside, hurrying to open as many windows in the kitchen as he could. There was no one there to greet him, and before he could shift in, he had to move stacks of boxes the previous priest had left into the garage. There was no room in the garage for his car by the time he was done.

On the kitchen table, under a biscuit tin, disappointingly empty, was a note from his predecessor, Father O'Keefe, welcoming him to the parish and explaining he would come and collect the boxes when he could. The house smelt of musty old carpet and cat pee. The note said the cat, Josiah by name, was with a neighbour and could he take care of her until he came up for the boxes.

He sighed, poured a glass of water and sat down fanning himself with a newspaper, intending to rest while he rehydrated, but the smell from under the fridge was too offensive. When he shifted it away from the wall, he found an accumulation of food scraps and rubbish accidentally dropped and never retrieved. He had been told Father O'Keefe had insisted on doing all his own housework. Wouldn't allow a woman into the presbytery. A moratorium, aimed at safeguarding his chastity.

He took his glass of water into the lounge and sat down. The smell of warm dust and mouldy curtains pervaded. He went over to open one of the single hung windows. It took an effort. The sash was broken and it crashed back down. He was looking for something to prop it up with when his phone sounded. His mother. He made the mistake of sharing with her the state of the presbytery.

In an attempt to jolly him up, Father Ward's mother drove all the way up from Auckland the following day with a box of cleaning agents and a determination to purge the house of bad odours, dust, cobwebs and everything else he had mentioned in his depressed state the night before. It was yet another reminder not to share his problems with mother. There was no point in accepting a parish at the other end of the island if he was going to involve her over the phone. Her close proximity to the cathedral where he had spent the first three years since ordination was a constant source of embarrassment. In the end, he had limited her visits to once a week when she arrived with tins of baking and a casserole dish with a meal she had prepared.

Dear mother, she was a good and generous soul, well-meaning and solicitous to a fault. Her son a priest. Just like her brother, God rest his soul. Her brother, Father Ward's Uncle Matt, had been an amiable, easy-going man, loved by his parishioners and looked up to by his nephew, Ian. He had been such a familiar, comfortable, happy presence during Ian's childhood that when other adults asked him what he wanted to be when he grew up, he could think of nothing better than being a priest himself. So, there was the answer to Father Gilbert's question.

When his uncle passed on, he left his gold-plated ciborium, breviary and vestments to Ian. Which had sealed the boy's fate in a sense, because thereafter there was never any question that Ian was to be a priest. He was bright enough. Pious enough. And certainly enthusiastic enough. However, his skill in dealing with people in a manner considered priest-appropriate was considered somewhat lacking. Nothing like the man in whose footsteps he aspired to follow.

During his first appointment at the cathedral, that particular weakness had not been called into question. Most of the congregation on any Sunday were tourists, without any inclination to build a relationship with the priest. The same could not be said about his first appointment as a sole charge parish priest, in an isolated part of the country, where parishioners were very keen to be on friendly terms with their priest.

He had been counselled in the seminary to cultivate a reserved manner, to be assertive and strong and curb his natural inclination to please and be agreeable; but in the absence of all friends, family and fellow priests that had proved difficult.

The parish priest he had served under while still training as a seminarian had been scathing in his report. 'Ian lacks male aggressiveness, has an undeveloped maleness, a softness and a lack of firmness and perseverance. He is oversensitive and his need to please is unsuitable for exerting authority.'

Lacks perseverance. It had confounded him then and it confounded him now. How on earth could that parish priest have formed such a judgement? Ian had argued it was based on speculation which then enabled him to dismiss the rest of the critique as specious as well. Still, the rector at the seminary had subsequently counselled him on the need for a greater assertion of his masculinity.

Father Gilbert stirred in his sleep and Father Ward put his hand to the teapot to see if it was still hot enough, but the old priest did not wake. He seemed a very relaxed man. Old and frail but possibly not the kind of man to find the Alexander family as daunting as he had. Looking back, Father Ward could see the first test of his assertiveness had been Mrs Alexander's visit to the presbytery one morning, after Mass. She came with produce from the family's farm: fresh eggs, vegetables, an abundance of stone fruit from her orchard and a large bag of grapes; and he had been effusive in his gratitude, inviting her in for a cup of tea.

"Oh thank you, Father, I was hoping for a quiet word." She sat erect on the edge of a seat in the lounge, clasping tightly her handbag, her legs crossed. She wore a hat, a tweed suit and chunky high-heeled shoes. A farmer's wife's Sunday best from a previous generation. There was no time to adapt to fashion in Mrs Alexander's agenda.

"Father, I wanted to talk to you about your sermon on Sunday."

"Ah, yes," said Father Ward, quietly pleased with his first effort, a sermon on Paul's call to love in his letter to the Corinthians.

"There was no mention of God or the good Lord

himself. Excuse me for saying so, Father Ward, but what you said could just as easily have been preached by some humanist. I don't need to remind you of the scripture, 'Seek ye first the kingdom of God and his righteousness and all these things shall be added unto you.' I mean the communists, the humanists and the Masons are all on about brotherhood and looking after each other, as though all we need is each other." She scoffed. "A cult of man with the grace of Christ as redeemer ignored. No mention of God with them either."

Father Ward put down his cup of tea. "I think it goes without saying God is love and the basis of all love, Mrs Alexander. I may not have stated that, but it was understood, don't you think?"

"Not to these people, Father. They need it spelled out clearly."

Father Ward hesitated.

"You're new to this aren't you, Father?"

"This is my first appointment as parish priest, Mrs Alexander," said Father Ward and paused, "but not my first parish." The tone was corrective and a little testy, but Mrs Alexander was not someone who conceded easily.

"You're very young," she said.

Father Ward stood up. It was time to be even more assertive "Was there anything else?"

Mrs Alexander ignored the hint and unclasped her handbag, withdrawing a book with a photo of Pope Paul VI. "I think you should read this. Pope Paul the sixth was all about the cult of man. Always on about the rights of man, ignoring God's rightful place, in the order of things. Did you know his parents were Free Masons? Look," she said and opened to a page showing the photo of a gravestone. "See at the bottom. The square and compass of Freemasonry. That marks the graves of Pope Paul the sixth's mother's family."

"I'll just take your cup, Mrs Alexander," said Father Ward, both hands now holding cups, making it impossible to take hold of the proffered book.

Mrs Alexander was not to be deterred. "I'll leave this with you," she said and placed it firmly on the kitchen table. "I'm not sure what they teach you in the seminary these days. Too much psychology and not enough of what counts I'm told. But be that as it may, this book will set you straight on the changes Pope Paul the sixth made to the sacred formulation of consecration." She closed her eyes in contempt. "God have mercy on his soul."

Father Ward had the back door to the presbytery open and was smiling lamely. It had gone against his nature to signal his disapproval of what Mrs Alexander was saying and he was proud of his firmness in showing her the door, but if he thought that was the end of it he underestimated Mrs Alexander. The visit was followed by letters. He remembered back to his formation in the seminary and the call to respect every member of a parish. No one to be dismissed or ignored. All to be treated with dignity and respect. He attempted to respond. 'The sacred formulation of consecration may have been altered by Pope Paul VI, but what merciful God, in his love, would deny his people his body, blood, soul and divinity because of an alteration in the formula, as though it was some spell, an incantation with all power resting in words alone.'

The letter that came back impressed Father Ward. Mrs Alexander seemed well informed. 'Pope Paul VI tampered with an eucharistic consecratory formula established by Christ himself. Changing it implied it needed fixing. He went against scripture and tradition as well as definitions laid by the ecclesiastical Magisterium of the church. Let me remind you, Father Ward, of Canon VI of the Council of Trent "*Si quis dixerit canonem missae continere errores. Ideoque abrogandum esse, anathama sit*. (If anyone says the canon of the Mass contains errors, and must therefore be abrogated, let him be anathema.)"

Mrs Alexander was certainly not someone anyone could dismiss lightly. She had the support of others. When Father Ward discreetly inquired, he discovered she was well thought of. 'Very holy' was the general opinion and so any thought of gaining an ally who would provide some form of emotional support seemed unlikely. In fact, when talking to the bishop, he was told she was not to be offended, that it was important she be kept on good terms; but, and here was the caveat Father Ward struggled with, she was not to be allowed to dominate.

Devout, fervent parishioners like the Alexanders were at one end of the spectrum and at the other were a group he was equally ill at ease with. Catholics who appeared in the pews once in a while as though Mass on Sunday was only something to attend if you were in the mood. He grouped them together with the lapsed Catholics who turned up at the presbytery door asking to have their child baptised.

Complete strangers he had never seen at Mass suddenly there requesting baptism for their child. It seemed odd until he learned of the excellent reputation of the Catholic primary school and the preference given to baptised Catholics. He had attempted to give credibility to this practice by pointing out the child needed to be brought up in the faith and required them to attend Mass regularly before the baptism. Mass attendance promptly came to an end immediately following the christening.

He consoled himself with the thought that if all those in the district who came from time to time turned up on one Sunday, there would not be enough room in the church. Despite that, Father Ward took absenteeism as a personal affront to his ministry. Yet, try as he may, he could not seem to create the wow factor in his sermons and improve regular attendance. Other priests simply wrote it off as a quirk of the area, not to be taken personally, but these comforters fell silent in the face of the statistics his parish was posting for applications for marriage annulments. Three in just one year. And that in spite of a stern sermon about the permanency of the married state. 'What God has joined together let no man tear asunder.' He had, in his own estimate, been forceful, assertive, and authoritative, coming down from the altar to repeat Christ's strong admonitions on the sanctity of marriage.

No one commented on the sermon. After Mass, they seemed embarrassed and in a hurry to leave. Perhaps he had gone too far in mentioning the devil. 'This is the devil's hour. Time is running out for him and he is desperate. And he knows as I know that there is no attack more powerful in its destructiveness than breaking up families. Husbands and wives stand firm. Be aware those negative thoughts about your spouse are coming from one of his minions. Be aware and pray for God's protection.'

Or was it the mention of being in love. 'Agreeing to take a man to be your husband or agreeing to take a woman to be your wife is first and foremost an act of the will. Feelings come and go. They are not to be relied on. There will be days when you feel great love for your spouse and days when you do not. What matters is that decision, that act of the will you professed publicly on your wedding day. The world will tell you it's all about feelings and if you're not feeling love it's time to trade in and get a new model. But that is not based on truth.'

To be fair to himself he was not sure if any of those subsequently seeking an annulment were there that day to hear his sermon. But he had stopped mentioning the devil and gone back to using a book of sermons to find his text. That at least did not result in being given the cold shoulder. Try as he might, he could not develop a carapace to deflect the slights that offended and hurt.

"Oh, Father that was a long sermon today. Ha ha ha."

"You should learn some Maori, Father. Father Ramero, he learnt the Maori for Mass in one week."

He could even take umbrage with the thoughtless comments of children. "Father, when's Father O'Keefe coming back? He used to play soccer with us. He was so cool." Though not all of their comments were thoughtless. Some were calculated. An older girl scoffingly referring to him as the Jesus-man. "Oh here comes the Jesus-man."

All the previous priests were remembered for something, even going back to Father Black from the very early days of the parish. "He could put the fear of God in you. No one preached on hell like Father Black."

Father Ward wondered what he would be remembered for. Not for sermons. Not for speaking Maori. Not for being a cool guy.

He had hoped he would be the priest they remembered for taking care of long overdue maintenance. Paint was peeling from the church, rust was forming on the roof – there were water marks on the ceiling where it was already leaking – and the carpet was threadbare and mouldy. In that, he ran headlong into the conservative spending of the parishioners who were on the finance committee. It was the irrational conservatism of those who feared poverty. Money was to be kept, hoarded and salted away for emergencies; certainly not spent, unless absolutely necessary.

A wealthy widow had left a sizeable endowment to the church. More than enough to cover all maintenance costs. It had been invested. Money earned from that investment could be spent but not the principal. He had argued the essential nature of certain maintenance. “No, we can’t allow that, Father. There’ll be nothing left for emergencies.”

He had pointed out the water marks on the ceiling.

“That can be patched up. No need for a new roof, Father.”

“And the carpet?”

“Better than most of *our* carpets, Father.”

“And the paint peeling from the weatherboards?”

“I suppose we could fundraise for that.”

“Fundraise? But we have the money.”

There was no way around the impasse with practical arguments. Father Ward tried another tack. “God has, through the goodness of this benefactor, given us the money for the work. It would be remiss of us not to use it. A lack of faith in His ability to provide more if we need more. After all, we’re talking about the Creator of the universe and this is His church."

"God takes care of them who take care of themselves, Father. Mustn't be relying on mana from heaven," replied the chairman of the finance committee.

Thinking he was being too mild-mannered and needed a more assertive, authoritative approach, he had almost lost his temper in front of the entire parish council at a meeting he had especially convened, with the finance committee invited, to make a plea for common sense.

"Look," he said when those he had expected to support him remained silent, "this is ridiculous! That dear woman left that endowment to be used. We are insulting her memory and her intention in giving it to us. And, what's more, if we're going to treat that gift in that way what hope have we of others following her example. Personally, I would not . . ." And here he paused to take breath and raise his voice, "would not bequeath anything to a parish who show an unwillingness to actually use it!"

But while he may have thought he had almost lost his temper, the word from his housekeeper, Mrs Gaffney, who reported all the parish gossip, was that he most definitely *had* lost his temper. And that was the problem with having a kind and agreeable nature. Any departure from it was perceived in exaggeratedly negative terms.

Mrs Gaffney also reported that his hurried departure from the Alexander home had also been source of gossip. "They say the Alexander boy went to attack you when you used holy water and you ran for it." The antics of the Alexander boy in Mass and his inability to deal with them were fast becoming the hallmark of what he could see would be his legacy.

Father Gilbert came suddenly into wakefulness and pushed the Lazy Boy into an upright position. "Ah, yes," he said, seeing the pot of tea he reached over to pour himself a cup, "must have dozed off." The tea was stone cold, but he drank it without comment. "So," he said declining the offer of a scone, disappointing when Ward wanted to get rid of them and allow Mrs Gaffney to remedy her mistake in a new batch as soon as possible, "what made you become a priest?"

"My uncle was a priest. Father Matthew Ryan"

"Of course. I knew Father Ryan A good priest." He brought his hands crashing down on the sides of his chair, stifled a yawn and stood. "I really must be off to bed." He paused at the doorway and turned. "You know I was here relieving years ago. A great little parish. Good to be back."

Father Ward nodded and wished him a good night's sleep.

Chapter Four

The bishop had been receiving complaints about Father Gilbert for months. Phone calls, texts, emails and now a letter endorsed by every other priest in the retirement home. A formal complaint about the behaviour of Father Peter Gilbert, whose antics had gone beyond the reach of reasonable tolerance and exceeded the bounds of indulgent charity. Playing Rachmaninoff loudly in the early hours of the morning being the proverbial straw.

The bishop's secretary, an Irish ex-patriot, Father O'Connor, responded to the bishop's stern look with a shrug of his shoulders. "I met with Father Peter as per your instructions and very politely and diplomatically conveyed your concern about the upset he was causing the other residents. He listened dutifully and respectfully and said what he has been saying ever since we retired him from parish duties."

"Oh for goodness sake, what's wrong with the man?" said the bishop, "What do the doctors say about his injuries?"

"He still gets around with a walking stick. The broken shoulder has not healed as well as they expected and he has restricted movements."

"Is he still turning up at local parishes offering to celebrate Mass?"

"He is."

"So he's still getting out and about?"

"Every day. Off early in the morning, back in time for dinner. Takes his breviary, his rosary beads and a bottle of holy water. Matron sees him on his rounds from time to time. Always dressed in his Roman collar, striking up conversations wherever he goes. Spends a lot of time sitting in the local parks saying his rosary. There have been reports of him coming out of the local pubs."

"He's back drinking?" The bishop's tone signalled shock at the prospect.

"No, he's in there talking to people, praying for them, hearing confessions, acting like he's the local parish priest."

"And how do we know all this?"

"Father Doolan, the actual parish priest, is complaining."

The bishop sighed.

"You could require him to stop," suggested Father O'Connor, "He'll honour his vow of obedience."

"Stop being a priest? On what grounds? Has any member of the public complained?"

"No. On the contrary. Word is, he's liked. Good man to yarn to. Tells a good story, says the publican, a Catholic himself. There's another possibility, John."

The bishop was listening.

"You need to go there and talk to him personally. He may listen to you. He wouldn't still be a priest if it wasn't for you and I doubt he'd relish going back to living the way he was when you found him."

The bishop rested his head in his hand and closed his eyes. The burden of office weighed heavily on Bishop John Morley. He was tired, troubled by insomnia and diabetes and wearied by the difficulty of managing priests, some of whom were eccentric, difficult and stubborn, set in their ways and loathe to change.

"Alternately, there is the matter of the problem up north."

The bishop collapsed back in his chair. There was a long pause until he slowly shook his head. "He's too old for that. Wouldn't have the strength or the stamina."

"I disagree. He walks for miles, lame as he is, and he still has that bone crunching handshake. Let's not forget he's first and foremost a missionary who worked in Lahore, Pakistan."

"Somewhat historical, Father."

"That gritty determination of his is still alive and present."

"Alright then," said the bishop, agreeing to meet with

Father Gilbert. The following morning he drove out to the priests' retirement home, where he was ushered into Gilbert's room. He was struck by its Spartan appearance. The television had been removed and virtually nothing had been added to the basic furnishings provided by the diocese, except an old sepia photograph of his mother on the chest of drawers, a prie-dieu and an old valve radio.

Father Gilbert's warm regard for his bishop was immediately apparent. He stood up from the only chair in the room, shook the bishop's hand vigorously and sat down on the room's single bed. He bent forward to turn off his radio, but the bishop raised his hand to stop him. "Shame to turn that off."

They sat without talking and listened to the second movement in Mozart's symphony for a clarinet quintet, the bishop with his eyes closed. When the music finished, he nodded in approval and Father Gilbert switched off the radio.

"Better than Rachmaninoff, wouldn't you say, Peter?"

"Rachmaninoff was a tortured soul who did not suffer rejection lightly."

"Yes but, Peter, in the early hours of the morning?"

"I struggle to sleep and can't choose what the concert programme offers."

The bishop had noted Father Gilbert's subtle innuendo and was not impressed. "You have not been rejected, Father Peter. I would be failing in my duty of care to send an elderly priest into a parish who is convalescing from serious injuries."

"Convalescing? With respect, Bishop, I walk miles every day. I'm back to full strength."

The bishop drew in a deep breath and turned his head. It was difficult to confront this priest. The enthusiasm and light in his eyes were not unlike a newly ordained curate's. He turned to face him. "To be honest, it was hoped you would grow to like it here, Peter. To like it and accept it may be time to retire and enjoy what years you have left."

"Enjoy? Here?" Father Gilbert slapped his knees and laughed loudly. "I have nothing in common with the priests here. They like to read, watch television and drink whisky. I read my breviary. Full stop. I find television mind numbing. And I don't drink."

The bishop paused to consider his response and Father Gilbert, warming to his theme, went on, "The big deal around here is what's being served for pudding at dinner. Oh, and Scrabble. Tuesday night is Scrabble night. Occasionally, we have someone come in and perform for us. A pianist. An amateur theatre group. Children from the school."

He sighed and went on, "As a missionary, I've been shot at, imprisoned, starved and laid low by tropical diseases more often than I can count, but I would gladly trade any of that for the boredom I find here, Bishop."

"But I understood you were out and about every day talking to people as a priest."

Father Gilbert sighed. "Visitation was never my specialty. I want to say Mass, preach, hear confessions and run sacramental programmes."

The bishop drew breath to speak and Father Gilbert stood and walked to the room's small window. He turned back to the bishop. "I struggle here, Bishop."

The bishop frowned and shook his head slowly.

Father Gilbert gently rapped his closed fist against

the windowpane. Then he sat back on his bed. "I don't feel at home here. That feeling of despair is creeping up on me again."

The two men sat in silence.

Father Gilbert turned to his bishop and opened his mouth to speak, thought better of it, then went ahead anyway, "I will not go gentle into that good night," he said.

The bishop recognised the quote. "Old age should burn and rave at close of day, eh, Peter?" quoted the bishop.

"Rage, rage against the dying of the light," continued Father Gilbert.

"Dylan Thomas was a relatively young man when he wrote that, Peter."

"He was a grave man, near death who saw with blinding light," countered Father Gilbert.

"Peter, you grow old . . . you grow old . . . you should wear the bottoms of your trousers rolled," said the bishop.

"Oh, your grace, everything turns sour when you sit and wait for the end."

The bishop threw up his hands. "I can't win, can I? I thought I was doing you a favour finding you a room here. I mean if it was me, I'd be very content. All those books I've wanted to read. Uninterrupted walks. The same bed every night. As it is some of the beds I'm forced to sleep in . . . Hard, unyielding instruments of torture. And if I was here, I could control my diet more. Get my diabetes under control."

"Let me do your job for you then, Bishop."

The bishop laughed. "I have more compassion for my priests than that."

There was a knock at the door. The matron was there with a tray of tea and biscuits. They thanked her and waited for her to withdraw.

The bishop took up the teapot and poured.

"Father Tim Leonard," said Father Gilbert, declining the offer of tea, "Father Cornelius Tierney, Father Francis Douglas, Father Patrick McMahon, Father Peter Fallon, Father John Henegan . . ."

The bishop sipped his tea and then interrupted. "Should I know these priests?"

"Columban martyrs. Killed for the faith. China, Korea, The Philippines, Peru, Myanmar. Twenty-four of them."

"And your point, Father?"

"These are the men, *the men*, in whose footsteps I follow. They were beaten, starved, shot and tortured for the faith. None of them lived long enough to see out their days drinking endless cups of tea in a priests' retirement village."

Father Gilbert paused a long moment and the bishop put down his cup of tea to speak but could see the emotion building in his friend did not brook any interference.

"I have shamed their legacy, John. And I still need to make amends."

The bishop opened his mouth to speak but was waved quiet.

"Let me finish, please, John. I've had my time off. All those lost years. I'm grateful to you for giving me a second chance. And I'm asking you now, pleading with you actually, give me back that chance and I promise you I will not let you down. Send me anywhere and I'll work harder than any priest half my age." He went to his closet and withdrew a faded, purple stole. "This stole belonged to Father Francis Douglas. Beaten, tortured and killed by the

Japanese for refusing to break the seal of confession. His mother gave it to me on the day of my ordination. It was the only thing of Frank's she had."

"Alright," said the bishop, "I was hoping it wouldn't come to this, but if you insist, if you insist, I have a job in mind. God forgive me if I have this wrong and anything happens to you."

"Where?"

"A young priest with his first parish. Probably too much too soon, but I don't have much choice these days. Father Ian Ward. You may know him."

"Is he related to Father Matt Ryan?"

"Yes, his uncle. He's certainly not Matt but a fine young priest nevertheless. Earnest. A little uptight perhaps but as I say he's earnest, wants to do well. He's had his usual run of problems and we've tried to steer him through, but I think he could do with an older priest like yourself there to support him."

Father Gilbert was nodding. "Only too happy to help if you think I can. Wasn't much of a young priest myself of course." He smiled ruefully.

"There's something else. He's asked for me to send someone with your special training, though of course it may be nothing as these things often are." The Bishop shared what Father Ward had told him of the Alexander boy.

"Seems likely," said Father Gilbert.

"That's what I discerned."

"Once more unto the breach, eh John?"

The bishop did not share Father Gilbert's gung-ho attitude. "I don't need to tell you what happened last time, Peter. It could be dangerous."

Father Gilbert was smiling, shaking the bishop's hand vigorously. "Thank you, Bishop, I won't let you down."

"I just hope I'm not letting *you* down, Peter."

Father Gilbert did not hear. He was pulling down his travelling bag. By the time the bishop reached his car, he had started packing and was singing the Galilee song, "So I leave my boats behind. Set my heart upon the deep. Follow you again, my Lord."

Chapter Five

Dean Collins had gravitated to the Far North from Auckland, along with hundreds of others grown tired of city living and in need of a change. He had heard it was a good place for someone like him to be unemployed as there were virtually no jobs on offer for someone of low skills. The Department of Work and Income Support had no choice but to pay out the unemployment benefit to men like Dean. Which suited him perfectly.

He had been in the area all summer, sleeping rough in an old abandoned shed near the beach, supplementing his diet with pipis, found in abundance, just over the sandhills from his free accommodation. He'd bought himself a cheap fishing rod and was also catching the odd snapper. Which saved him money on food, allowing more for Old Pale Gold sherry and Ruby Red port when he went into town for supplies. Life was good for Dean. A huge improvement on sleeping under Grafton Bridge, down in Auckland. No police moving him on. No trouble from others sleeping rough.

He was in town and, having finished buying his supplies, was eating a pie when he happened to see Father Gilbert walking along on the other side. The priest caught his attention. You didn't see priests walking around these days. Dean couldn't recall the last time he'd seen one, well one he could see was a priest. It wasn't usual to see a priest dressed like one anymore. Back in the day, when they did, they used to be good for a few bucks. Dean watched him. He was old and seemed a bit lame in one leg. He couldn't be bothered crossing the road and hitting him up. Besides he had a sugar sack full of groceries. Hardly a good look when you wanted someone to think you were broke.

The priest happened to glance across the road and see him and, for a moment, their eyes locked. Just one brief instant. But it was enough for something deep down in the alcohol-fogged memory of Dean Collins to register and it made him sit up. He knew that priest and could have sworn the old priest knew him too. Only he wasn't letting on. He was walking away. Walking a little quicker than before, as though he was trying to put distance between them.

Dean stood up, craning forward, shifting around to follow the priest's progress through the other pedestrians. There was definitely something familiar about him. Who the hell was he? Dean didn't know any priests. Hadn't even seen a priest in years. Who the hell was he?

"I know that bugger. I know him," Dean muttered to himself. The priest had disappeared and Dean sat down. "That face. That face. I know that face. I know that face. Who the hell is he?"

Father Gilbert had no such trouble recalling who

Dean Collins was. He had no intention of making himself known to him and, watching him, from inside a coffee shop take up his sugar bag and walk north out of the town, he breathed a sigh of relief and took his coffee out onto the pavement to sit on a chair. Outside on the street, he was better able to observe, something he had learned to do in the missions, a way of checking the pulse of a place by watching the comings and goings of people in their place of commerce.

He had not had the time for this luxury on his last visit to the parish and had traded solely on the town's reputation in the media. High unemployment and a high ratio of Maori to European. At one time, in the early nineties it was known as the murder capital of New Zealand. Ten murders in six years. It was hard to match the reputation with what he was seeing now.

People seeing him there nodded and smiled. Some stopped to talk. There was none of the stress, urgency and purpose of a city. Some of these people were very laid back. A man walking the pavement in nothing but a pair of shorts, others in bare feet and some in gumboots. Gumboots on a hot February morning. An old man walked by in a shredded suit with tears in the pants and sleeves. Later a woman strolled by in bare feet with a tear in the back of her dress showing her underpants.

There was an air of carelessness and indifference to normal dress sense, with extremes that took Father Gilbert by surprise. Another woman walked by in her pyjamas. And the longer he sat there and saw the same people going back and forth, the clearer it became that these people weren't here to shop, they were here to wander and socialise. And they were only too happy to talk. Anything, it seemed, to break the long monotony of an existence with nothing to do but wander around town.

They contrasted with other groups. Young women in trouser suits and high heels holding takeaway coffee cups walking briskly back to the office from their breaks. Full of purpose and intent.

Tourists keeping close together while taking in as much as they could without seeming to, ready to file a report back home on the unusual inhabitants of this small town at the far end of this island nation, where so many people live without jobs and parade their poverty and aimlessness around for all to see.

Buskers singing from every corner. A Maori with a full facial tattoo, a straw hat and gumboots strumming furiously on a ukulele. A young woman singing outside the post office in full voice, a glorious, true voice, with an amazing range, amplified by the buildings and heard up and down the street. It was a good place to have a coffee on a warm, deep-blue-sky day. A relaxed, friendly town where people were free to be whoever they wanted.

And on the fringes, signs of the menace one would expect in a country's murder capital. Emaciated methamphetamine addicts, with dull, empty eyes walking by. Young men in loud, souped-up American import cars, their arms slung out the doors, music booming from their sound systems, showing off their drug money and happy to offer something to break the monotony of the lost souls.

Some walking by gave him a nod of acknowledgement. Others wished him a good morning. And some Catholics stopped to talk and introduce themselves.

Time passed and he was surprised to look at his watch and see it was lunch time.

As he stood up to leave, he was greeted by an elderly couple, Mary and Michael Finnerty, who were delighted to see him. He remembered them well from his last time in the parish. "How are you both?"

"As good as can be expected, Father. Mary has a pacemaker and I'm on my second hip. Hard on hips all those years on a farm."

"Still together," said Mary, beaming. "Fifty years last week, Father."

"Well done."

"No well done you, Father. We haven't forgotten what you did for us," said her husband.

"Michael," said Father Gilbert, "it was all your own doing. I just pointed out the obvious."

"Even so, you'll always be a guest of honour at our place."

It was a gratifying encounter and Father Gilbert made his way back to the presbytery in good spirits. He found Father Ward pouring over bank statements, in preparation for a meeting with the parish finance committee. "The finance committee likes a full account of all expenditure," he explained, "they are very scrupulous."

Concern with parish finances had never taken much of Father Gilbert's time. His frugal habits had stood him in good stead in the face of any close scrutiny and, in his opinion, there were more pressing matters to contend with.

Father Ward politely inquired how his walk had been.

"Too much to pray for in this town to have Mass just

twice during the week," was Father Gilbert's response. "I'd like to reinstate daily Mass."

Father Ward was ready for this. "The parishioners are only interested in coming twice a week. The only person who came on Tuesdays and Thursdays was an old man who has since died. Saturdays are all about sport in this town."

"Be that as it may, I'd like to celebrate Mass every day, providing you have no objection."

"Of course not," said Father Ward and immediately wished he hadn't. The matter had been decided by the parish council and endorsed by the bishop. He had missed an opportunity to be assertive.

"And have you any objection to my preaching on the Blessed Eucharist this Sunday?"

Father Ward, for whom sermons were a weekly ordeal, agreed without any reservations. The rest of the week proved quiet and uneventful. Father Gilbert said Mass on his own on the Thursday and concelebrated with Father Ward on Wednesday and Friday, after which he went off each morning for a walk down the town. He assisted Father Ward during the rest of the day in whatever way he could.

Mrs Alexander was there at Mass on Wednesday and Friday and gave assurances that her son Mark was not causing any trouble, well not to the extent he had been. He was keeping to himself and staying up all hours but was not as abusive. The following Sunday when Mr and Mrs Alexander turned up for Mass, again without the troublesome Mark, Father Ward's inquiries still found no further need for concern. He mentioned this to Father Gilbert as the two were vesting for Mass. "Not unusual. He's waiting for me to leave. But rest assured, Father, I'm not going anywhere."

This was not the assurance Father Ward was looking for.

As the congregation filed into the church, they were greeted by the organist playing Saint Thomas Aquinas's *Godhead here in Hiding.* Some of them were able to recall the lyrics as they waited for Mass to begin. 'Godhead here in hiding whom I do adore. Masked by these bare shadows, shape and nothing more. Seeing, touching, tasting are in thee deceived. How says trusty hearing? That shall be believed. What God's son hath told me take for truth I do. Truth himself speaks truly or there's nothing true.' And in a departure from the norm, Father Gilbert used these words as the basis of his sermon.

"*Adore te devote, latens Deitas*," he said. An old priest, whom many had never seen before beginning his sermon in Latin. It was surprising, but not to Mrs Alexander and those of her age for whom it provoked a pleasing nostalgia. "Godhead here in hiding whom I do adore," she said quietly to herself and Father Gilbert, hearing her, congratulated Mrs Alexander and asked her to repeat aloud for others to hear.

"Godhead here in hiding," she said.

Father Gilbert smiled his appreciation. "Saint Thomas Aquinas's words from the hymn your wonderful organist played while you came in this morning. 'Godhead here in hiding.'" He pointed to the tabernacle and turned back to the congregation. "Good morning everyone, for those who don't know me, my name is Father Gilbert. Lovely to be back in your parish.

"Father Ward has kindly allowed me to preach on the

Blessed Eucharist this morning. The Blessed Eucharist, the very heart and substance of my existence, the reason I get up in the morning, the reason I am a priest." He stopped and turned to the tabernacle again. "A small wafer of bread in which the body, blood, soul and divinity of Our Blessed Lord is present, something that has been changed into someone," he said and turned back. "To one who has faith, no explanation is necessary. To one who does not have faith, no explanation is possible." To quote Saint Thomas Aquinas once again.

"I am not here to explain. I simply want to point out what we should be seeing through the eyes of faith. For make no mistake, without the eyes of faith there is nothing to see. *Visus, tactus, gustus in te fallitur*. The physical senses of seeing, touching and tasting are deceived. But God's son has said it is so and therefore we believe. 'What God's son hath told me take for truth I do. Truth himself speaks truly or there's nothing true.'

"But imagine, if you will, what we would see if He was not masked by bare shadows, in the shape of a small piece of bread and nothing more. Imagine what some of our dear saints have been privileged to see.

"We would see a blinding light, radiating from the host, the brightness of which would light up the whole of this church; beams of it descending upon the town in shafts so luminous people would stop and shield their eyes. Work in the town would come to a standstill.

"We would hear choirs of heavenly angels singing His praises. Handel's *Messiah*. Leonard Cohen's *Hallelujah*. David's secret chord laid bare in a rhapsody of harmony and joy so loud and pure everyone who heard it would be frozen to the spot, their eyes closed in ecstasy. Can you imagine? Let yourself try. And hear the sound of thunder as countless angels sing. Throngs of them descending and ascending, all around the altar, in adoration of God's son here present, body, blood, soul and divinity."

He paused and shook his head. "Words," he said and sighed, "as Alfred Lord Tennyson rightly said, 'they half reveal and half conceal.' What we need is that soul-expanding crescendo of a cinematic musical score as it swells and swells, until all the strings and the orchestra's entire brass section are pouring forth."

Father Gilbert turned to the tabernacle, raised his arms, hung his head and closed his eyes for a long moment. Then he turned back to face the congregation.

"My dear people, let us be thankful God in his wisdom is here in hiding, masked by these bare shadows, shape and nothing more. Can you imagine the pandemonium that would ensue if He allowed himself to be seen in all his glory? The transfiguration right here above this small provincial town. There would be traffic jams in and out of the town and crowds and crowds of people filing up to the church. And those within the church? Your good selves. Oh, you would be so envied and admired for having been this close to the Creator of the Universe, in all his glory.

"To be here, as you are today, to be sure of a seat, you would have to sleep outside overnight. Commerce in the town would come to a halt each time a priest offered the sacrifice of the Mass. The sound of the heavenly choirs would make anything else impossible. Satellites would record an intense bright light emanating from this church, visible from outer space. This church, this town, this whole region would be transformed. Nothing would ever be the same. You would not be the same.

"So let us be grateful to God, He who dwells in unapproachable light, that He has protected us from all that. As the Cure of Ars once said, if we knew the value of the Mass we would die of joy. But let us not forget what we have just imagined either. For that is what we are asked to see through the eyes of faith. That is the reality here in this Catholic church. God's greatest miracle. His son, present on the altar. King of kings. Lord of hosts. Beloved son of the Father. Light of the World.

"As I said in my opening remarks, the Eucharist is the reason I get up in the morning. The reason I am a priest. I could talk about the Eucharist all morning but I won't." He smiled. "So let me finish with one story and an invitation. There are many miracles associated with the Eucharist and books have been written about them. In an effort to debunk the mystery of one of these miracles, the miracle of a bleeding host, a scientist took a small sample to his laboratory. After extensive examination, he concluded it was definitely human tissue, only it was unlike any tissue he had ever seen before. 'The genome,' he said, 'is extraordinary. It is as if this human being is without any human ancestor, as though he is the first and only of his kind. There are simply no genes, no basis for this human's traits other than himself." He paused to let that find room in their thoughts and then he extended his arms.

"My dear people, Father Ward has reduced the number of Masses for a very simple reason. No one was coming. While I am here, Father has agreed to let me say Mass every day and I invite you to join me. There is no more powerful form of prayer. As Padre Pio once said, the world could exist more easily without the sun than the Mass. And the world needs your prayers at this hour in its history more than ever before. Your town needs your prayers at this hour more than ever before."

He concluded with Saint Thomas Aquinas's *Panis Angelicus*. "May the bread of Angels become bread for mankind. The bread of heaven puts all foreshadowing to an end. Oh thing, miraculous! The body of the Lord will nourish the poor, the servile and the humble."

The next day, Monday, two people turned up to Mass. Two. Father Gilbert reminded himself of Thomas a Kempis's words. 'Be not angry that you cannot make others as you wish them to be since you cannot make yourself as you wish to be.' It was a start, he told himself, and was full of praise for the two people and the wisdom of their choice. He went back to the presbytery for what Father Ward, who had gone off for the day, had told him would be a quiet morning on his own and a moment later there was a loud, insistent knock on the back door. A demanding, disrespectful knock. Someone needing a lesson in manners.

Father Gilbert opened the door to a hunched, misshapen creature, with one leg shorter than the other and a deformity at the top of his spine. He was reminded of Verdi's Rigoletto, the hunch backed jester. When the small man of indeterminate age swung his head up to look him in the eye, there did seem the same mocking intent of Rigoletto.

"Haaaloo," said the man. The voice was odd, too, the voice of the handicapped and deformed who live alone and, without the banter of others, develop a voice register that can only be described as unnerving.

Father Gilbert did not respond.

“Halloo,” repeated the man, “my name’s William. Where’s the other priest?”

“He’s gone out for the day.”

“Oh,” said William, studying Father Gilbert. “Well, he usually gives me twenty dollars. My benefit’s not due and I’m out of money, see. I got nothing and me benefit’s not due today. I need money for something to eat.”

“Twenty dollars?” said Father Gilbert.

“Yees,” said William, smiling ingratiatingly. Charles Dickens’ Uriah Heap came to mind.

“And what do you do for Father Ward?”

“Do?” William was puzzled. His tone was whiney and irritated.

Father Gilbert gave a slight smile. “I don’t want to just give you something for nothing. Where’s the dignity in that?”

“Oh, I don’t mind,” said William quickly.

“And I haven’t that kind of money to just give away. I tell you what I’ll do. You do some weeding for Father and I’ll fix you something to eat.”

“Weeding?”

“Yes,” said Father Gilbert, coming out of the presbytery and closing the door behind him. “Weeding. I’ll show you.”

William followed slowly, dragging one leg after the other. He arrived at the flower bed Father Gilbert was standing beside, seemingly out of breath from the exertion, a pained expression on his face.

Father Gilbert went into the implement shed for some tools. When he re-emerged William was gone, moving quickly down the drive.

He had not been back in the presbytery a minute when the phone was ringing.

"Is that you, Father? Mrs Wainui here."

Before Father Gilbert could identify himself, the woman launched into a complaint. "That holy water you gave me is no good. That bloody kehua is still here. Keeping me up at night. Sprayed everywhere with that stuff. Useless. Still banging around all night. I'm getting a kaumatua to do the job. Useless," she repeated and the phone went dead.

"Yes, you do that," said Father Gilbert to himself and replaced the receiver.

With a pot of tea brewing, Father Gilbert spread lashings of marmalade on his toast and sighed in happy anticipation as he raised it to his mouth just as the phone rang again. This time the caller allowed Father Gilbert to identify himself.

"Oh, the new priest," said the caller in a Dutch accent, "I'm glad I caught you. You may be able to help me. I don't seem to be getting anywhere with Father Ward. I'm forming a committee and I want Father to be a part of it. It's very important work. We're going to reform the priesthood. It's long overdue and we've so much work to do."

Father Gilbert listened at length, not sure if the man was *compos mentis*, but electing to give him the benefit of the doubt. When he finally drew to a conclusion, he said, "Look, why don't you write all that down and submit it to Father for his consideration because I think you've made some good points."

This suggestion was met with a hesitant response, but Father Gilbert pressed on about the importance of documentation and the man signed off, without much enthusiasm for the task ahead. The pot of tea was now lukewarm and he was putting the kettle on again when the front door bell sounded. "*Non est pax impiis*, (No rest for the wicked)" he said and, hoping for a quick resolution to what awaited, placed two fresh pieces of bread in the toaster and engaged it. The caller this time was a tall, broad-shouldered, handsome young man with a winning smile. Father Gilbert recognised him from Mass the day before. "Hello, Father. Greg Belich. Can I have a word?"

Chapter Six

Father Ward arrived home that evening full of praises for the beauty of the New Zealand bush. He had been on a hike to see Tane Mahuta. "At one stage," he said, "the others left me and I was all alone, nothing but the sound of bellbirds and tui, and then they moved on, too. I was completely alone. Not a sound and you know I was so struck by the majesty and silence of that bush. It was like being in a cathedral. And the beauty of the place, untouched by man, in its original God created state . . . It was quite a spiritual experience I have to say."

"The world is charged with the grandeur of God. There lives the dearest freshness deep down things," said Father Gilbert.

Father Ward was nodding in agreement. "Gerard Manly Hopkins."

Father Gilbert smiled. They had eaten their evening

meal and were seated in the lounge sharing their day.

"We had a visitor today," said Father Gilbert. "Said his name was William. He wanted money."

"Oh, yes," said Father Ward, frowning.

"I offered him work in exchange and couldn't see him for dust."

Father Ward laughed. "When age is in the wit is not out it seems."

"Then the phone started ringing. You have some intriguing people in your parish. A man phoned to ask if you had decided to be part of a committee for the reform of the priesthood."

"That would be Theo. Unusual fellow. Suddenly turned up in the parish and then started hounding me about the reform of the priesthood."

"How do you find him?"

"Well, the idea of asking me a priest to reform other priests seems ill considered, but he makes some good points."

"Mmm," Father Gilbert agreed. "I formed the same impression. Anyway, I asked him to write everything down for your consideration. That always tests the resolve of these people. Most of them don't."

Father Ward nodded his approval. "Thank you," he said.

"A few minutes later, there was another visitor at the door. A young man seeking an annulment."

"What?" said Father Ward, clearly not impressed. "That's five, now." Father Gilbert was curious to know about the other four.

"One seems a genuine case. A man forced into a

loveless marriage to a young woman after she fell pregnant. He's likely to find a sympathetic ear from the Marriage Tribunal. Not the others. Not the others."

"Have you tried to change their minds?"

"I doubt they would be open to that."

"Invite those four to the presbytery anyway," said Father Gilbert, "they can always refuse."

Two did refuse. But one, a young man who had been married seven years, and had, to use his words, 'fallen out of love and found someone else' could not refuse a priest and agreed. He was the son of devout Catholic parents and was motivated to seek an annulment in deference to their wishes. His parents also happened to own the large farm he managed and would not bequeath it to him if he was not willing to do what was right in the eyes of the church. The other man came with a Filipino woman who would not consent to marry him without an annulment.

When they arrived at the presbytery they were introduced to Mary and Michael Finnerty and John Kildaire whom Father Gilbert had also invited.

The wives of the men seeking annulment seemed happy to be there. They sat together, apart from their husbands, open to what was being offered. Everyone in the room knew each other and there was some informal chat though the feeling was strained and they were pleased when Father Gilbert made a start.

"What God has joined together, let no man tear asunder," he said. Father Ward's eyes widened and he shifted uncomfortably, aware of the reaction of the two husbands. "The words of Our Blessed Lord himself," Father Gilbert continued. "Words the church takes very seriously."

He paused. "Canon law does, however, allow for annulments on certain grounds. Such as, did the couple freely enter into the contract? Did they intend to be married for life? Were they open to children? Did they intend to be faithful? There are others. But it is a long and difficult process taking your case to the Tribunal and certainly not something to enter into lightly."

Father Gilbert nodded to the elderly couple sitting on the couch together. "Let me introduce you to Michael and Mary Finnerty. Fifteen years ago, Michael and Mary sought an annulment from the church. I was in the parish at the time and I asked them here today to share their story with you." He nodded to Michael and Mary who looked at each other.

"You go first," said Mary.

The elderly gentleman came forward in his seat and nodded to everyone. "Good morning," he said, "Not one for talking really, not in front of people, so bear with me." He cleared his throat. "I was recently retired and was spending more time at home with Mary. We'd sold the farm and moved into town. We were getting on each other's nerves." He paused and looked to his wife.

"It was difficult for both of us," said Mary. "Michael was very picky, telling me what needed doing around the house. He was annoyed when my friends came over to talk, said they stayed too long and went on and on about nothing. I've always been patient but it was getting a bit much."

Mary looked to her husband who smiled encouragement. "Michael's been a farmer all his life, a good farmer. And suddenly he had no farm to manage, nothing to organise and I felt he was trying to organise me in a way that wasn't respectful. Eventually, I wasn't feeling any warmth towards him. I was happiest when he left the house. I remember thinking this was not the man I married and then I wondered if I actually knew the man I'd married. We'd never spent so much time together you see and I questioned whether I really loved this man."

Michael had his arms folded. The memory was bitter, but he took up the story. "One day it came to a head. There was shouting and awful words were exchanged and, well it was me, I suggested maybe we weren't meant for each other anymore, and Mary didn't disagree. I called in to see Father here. Our parish priest was away at the time.

"Father Gilbert wanted a meeting. And like today he'd invited others to share their story. Basically these people said, hey you're not alone, we've been through rocky patches but hang in there, talk it out, get help, make changes, don't give up on forty years together. And we listened. One of the people who talked that day was John." He nodded in the direction of the man who had come on his own. "He and his wife had been divorced and he just kept saying it was the biggest mistake they ever made. John's a friend of mine and I took that seriously.

"When Father got in touch and asked me to come today, he asked me if I still loved Mary." He laughed. "I told him I did and then he asked me why. I came up with the usual lines, all borrowed from movies and books I suppose. That's why I stopped myself, Father and asked you for time to think about it."

"And have you?"

"It's taken me a few days but . . . yeah."

"Can you tell Mary?"

"Sure." He clasped his wife's hand and smiled. "First

of all, Mary, I love you because when I look into your eyes like I am now I just see so much love, love for me that goes on and on. No end to it. I know what I'm like, I can be grumpy, inconsiderate, impatient, slow to forgive and demanding, but that love never goes away.

"But I don't just love you because you love me, Mary. I love you because you complete me. Now that sounds like something from a book too, I know, but after plenty of thought I can't think of a better way to put it. When you're not around, Mary, I'm full of worry and fear and second guess everything I think. But with one word from you I'm whole and all that negative stuff is sent packing.

"Finally, with you, I can do anything I put my mind to. Because you believe in me, I believe in myself. And why wouldn't I? You're smart and wise and full of common sense. When you say I can do something I know it must be true." He let go of his wife's hands and sat back in his chair.

"Thank you," said Mary.

"And, Mary, do you have an answer to that question?" asked Father Gilbert.

"Oh yes, I tell him all the time. He's my big bear, makes me feel safe." She paused and smiled. "Michael's better with words than me. He's an all-round charmer." She laughed. "When I first fell in love with him, I remember he had this twinkle in his eyes. I thought it was just for me, but I learned later that Irish charm was for everyone."

"Hey," said Michael, "there's charm and there's charm."

She laughed. "Michael," she said turning to him, "I love you so much. I can't imagine life without you."

There was a collective sigh from the other two

women.

"Oh, just one other thing, Father. Part of my loving Michael is not feeling any love for him sometimes. But as you taught us, Father, love is a decision, an act of the will that does not depend on feelings. They come and go. Two more things actually. I just want to say to you young people. Those exercises Father will give you. They're important. They were really helpful to Michael and I."

"We'll get to those," said Father Gilbert looking at his watch. "Shall we take a short break for a coffee."

One of the husbands seeking an annulment sighed. "Can't spend too long, got to get back to work."

Father Gilbert nodded to John Kildaire who took a breath and started in on his story.

"About fifteen years ago now, I came back to the Catholic church. I'm a recovering alcoholic and when I joined Alcoholics Anonymous they told me I needed a Higher Power. I was raised a Catholic so the God they had taught me as a kid was the only Higher Power I knew. So it seemed right I come back to church. Father Gilbert was here at the time. Only passing through as it turned out, but he was the one who was here to greet me and I recognised him. We went to school together down there at Sacred Heart back in the day. He invited me to call by and so I did. He knew I'd been married and asked what had happened to my wife, thinking she was deceased. I told him no she wasn't deceased she was alive and well, married to another man in Australia. He wanted to know what happened, so I told him. He invited me here today to tell my story again.

"Cheryl and I had been married twenty-five years. Three great kids. All grown up and left home. And it was down to just us. I had a good job and everything seemed fine until one day, Cheryl confronted me about my drinking. She'd had enough of me coming home late at night smelling of alcohol.

"That took me by surprise. Drinking was part of the job. A way of getting to know clients and de-stressing with work mates before coming home. I didn't have a problem. It was Cheryl who had the problem. She didn't know how lucky she was. A husband with a good job. Neither she nor the kids had ever wanted for anything. I was furious. Her telling me I had a problem. It was outrageous. And I told her she was no fun anymore. That she needed to get a life and stop trying to spoil mine.

"That didn't go down too well and the atmosphere around home was icy for a while. I didn't want to go home. I stayed out later. I remember thinking, I'll show her what a problem drinker is all about. Like I was punishing her. But really I just used her as an excuse to shrug off all restraints and start drinking to my heart's content.

"Cheryl wasn't the kind of woman to tolerate that and it wasn't long before she gave me an ultimatum which was basically: her or the drink. We hadn't had relations for a long time. Hard when you're drunk. And to me, at that stage, she was just the grumpy woman who was trying to stop me having a good time. I remember thinking there were plenty more where she came from. One of the women at work seemed keen on me and there were others I was keen on myself. I told her if she wanted to go then go and good riddance. I had no idea what I was doing really. I was that out of touch with who I really was and what I really needed in my life. They say an alcoholic is incapable of real love, and it's true. I was in love with the booze. That's what occupied all my thoughts. That's what I looked forward to. Cheryl was just a nuisance getting in the way.

"Anyway, true to her word, Cheryl left me. Got the shock of my life. Came home to a silent house. No meal in the oven. A note on the table. She wasn't a Catholic. Had been married in the church and was happy to bring the children up Catholic, but she had no qualms about a divorce. And there it was in the note. She was filing for divorce, gone off to her mother's. And that's when the drinking really took off.

"Without Cheryl at home taking care of things, my world fell to pieces quickly. Bills weren't being paid. The house smelt of booze. Empty fast-food containers bulged out of rubbish bins. The house was soon a mess. I was going to work in un-ironed shirts. But worse than all that, I'd lost my soul mate, the one who had really cared about me. I mean *really* cared. The one I could talk to about anything and know I'd be listened to. The one who cooked my favourite meals. The one who kept me up to date with the kids and the grandchildren. The one who knew all their birthdays. The one who kept in touch with my parents and my siblings and . . . all my relations really. The one who gave me backrubs when I couldn't sleep at night. The one who did all the grocery shopping and always stocked up on my treats. The list just goes on and on.

"Eventually I lost my job and was in a desperate state." He paused and nodded ruefully. "Anyway, the long and the short of it is I gave up the booze, got help, did what Cheryl had been asking me to. But it was too late to get her back. She had another life. I found that out when I tracked her down. I knew I'd lost the only woman I was going to love and you know what she said to me when I told her that. She told me she felt the same. Sure she was happy with her new husband but the love she and I had once shared was not there. We'd both treated something very precious too cheaply. And that's my story," he concluded and nodded to Father Gilbert.

It was an abrupt ending and no one spoke. Realising there was something more needed, John spoke again, "I live alone now. And if there's one thing I'd say to you," he said pausing to look the two men in the eye. "Be careful. It's so easy to throw a marriage away these days. Everyone seems to be doing it, right? But soul mates, that person you fell in love with, that person who was the centre of your world, are not easily replaced. All marriages go through hard times. Calling it quits is not the answer."

Father Gilbert could see one of the estranged husbands was restless and had begun checking texts on his phone but he pushed on, outlining the exercises he wanted both couples to complete before they met again for a follow-up. Then they all took their leave.

The last to leave were Michael and Mary. Michael sighed at the effusiveness of Father Gilbert's gratitude and exchanged a look with his wife.

"Is everything alright with you two?" asked Father Gilbert.

"Yes, yes," said Michael quickly, and then belatedly, "we're fine."

"And the family?"

Michael opened his mouth to speak but thought better of it.

Father Gilbert looked to Mary for some enlightenment. She was attempting to cover the sadness in her eyes with a smile and was ushering her husband to the door.

Father Gilbert paused at the front door after he had closed it. He went back into the lounge where Father Ward was waiting. "The wives seemed open, but their husbands . . . One of them seemed almost hostile to what John Kildaire was saying towards the end, as though he thought John was being patronising. And the other one seemed distracted the whole time. You must have seen the way he checked the messages on his phone when Michael Finnerty was talking. To be honest, Peter, I don't hold out much hope."

"We'll see," said Father Gilbert, "your prayers and mine. Point is, we've planted a seed. We've done something. And those exercises are well designed. They have to write their response and then read them, uninterrupted, to their spouses. That usually has them talking afterwards. We need to pray those exercises rekindle what's been lost."

Father Ward folded his arms. "I *have* been praying," he said and sighed.

"Good, because make no mistake, Ian, this is a spiritual battle we're in. Those young couples think the problem is each other. It's not. Their real enemy is spiritual. When Cardinal Carlo Carfarra established the Marriage and Family studies all those years ago, he was having so much opposition and difficulty, he wrote to Sister Lucia, one of the children from Fatima, a nun at the time.

"He asked for her prayers and what she wrote back has always stuck with me. She told him the decisive battle between Our Lord and Satan will be over marriage and the family, and that anyone who works for the sanctity of marriage and the family will most certainly experience difficulty. It makes sense.

"Man is the highest point of God's creation and so it follows a man and woman in love is the ultimate expression of God's love on Earth. If Satan can't attack God he's going after married couples, make no mistake. And when the wolf attacks the sheep, the shepherd does all he can."

Father Ward was not comfortable with Father Gilbert talking of Satan. It smacked of a former time when priests focussed too much on the devil and not enough on God's love; and the following Saturday, while preparing his sermon, during Father Gilbert's absence, he decided he would use the Gospel for Sunday to make his point.

Chapter Seven

The following morning after Mass, Father Gilbert went off to visit Mary and Michael Finnerty. It was a warm summer's morning and he found them at the front of their home working together on a climbing rose. Mary was busy pruning and Michael was extending the trellis. They immediately dropped tools at the sight of the priest pulling into their drive and invited him in for a coffee.

Mary praised his good timing as she checked on a banana cake in the oven and declared it ready. Patting his stomach and turning his head, Father Gilbert made a good show of declining even the offer of a small slice until Michael cut himself a large wedge, covered it in lashings of butter and closed his eyes in ecstasy as he took pleasure in another of his wife's wonderful specialties.

"Just a small piece," said Father Gilbert and, taking a bite, he was instantly under the spell of Mary's culinary skills. He followed one small piece with several other small pieces. And any pride he felt in finally being able to say no was put on hold when Mary cut half of what remained and insisted he take it with him.

They talked about the dry summer and water restrictions and the wonderful condition of Father Gilbert's Ford and Mary's baking and Michael's obvious ability to maintain a trim waistline despite that.

"Most of Mary's baking is for the grandchildren," said Michael, pointing out photos of children adorning the kitchen sideboard which Mary went through proudly naming them all, with Michael commenting on some aspect of each one's personality, something he neglected to do with the three children in the last of the photos.

The omission was so obvious something needed to be said. Mary's eyes teared up and she started clearing the table of cups and plates.

"We don't have much to do with those three, Father, it's a bit of a sore point."

Father Gilbert nodded.

"You were right to think there was something wrong yesterday, Father, I . . . Well, to be honest I felt like a bit of a fraud, spouting off how much I loved my wife and giving the impression we were the wonderful Catholic couple you paraded in front of others as an example."

Father Gilbert raised his eyebrows.

"I know," said Michael, "it wasn't really like that but

that's how it felt. Truth is we may still be married but I don't think we've done such a good job with our children. Only two out of five go to Mass, at least last time we checked. They could've dropped off too. And we haven't done a very good job of dealing with one of our daughter-in-laws. We always knew it would be difficult. There was that cultural difference. She's from Hong Kong. Her mother was Chinese and her father was British. Extremely wealthy. Her parents divorced when she was young. It was messy. She was badly hurt. Has nothing to do with them now. We had the idea that things would work out if we were loving and kind enough. And for a while it did work that way, didn't it, Mary?"

Mary sighed. "I'm sure Father doesn't want to hear all this."

"I'm fine with it," said Father Gilbert, "but that's up to you."

"Mary?" Michael wanted his wife's approval.

"Go ahead, Michael, we could do with another perspective," she said, bearing herself up and forcing a smile as she wiped her eyes with a tissue.

"The loving approach worked reasonably well until one day they asked us to pay the deposit on a house they wanted. We asked all the reasonable questions and it seemed like a good prospect. At the time, it was a way for them to get into the housing market and my son assured us we would be paid back when he sold the house at a profit and bought another one. But then they changed their minds and said they wouldn't be selling. They wanted to keep it. Mary and I talked long and hard about this and, given their record with money, decided against paying the deposit. They were very disappointed and we weren't allowed to see our grandchildren.

"A few years later, they approached us again. Another house. They wanted us to go guarantor and put our house up as collateral. We visited the property way out in the country and gave the request very serious consideration. My son was earning a huge salary but hadn't saved anything and there seemed little chance of him being able to service a big mortgage with the kind of lifestyle they lived. They were always off to Australia or Fiji on holiday, so we said no. Maybe that was wrong, Father. I don't know. But the risk of losing our house was scary. As it turned out, the way house prices have gone up, we would have been alright. But you don't know these things.

"And then they asked us for help to pay off a big credit card bill. They wanted a loan and said they would give us ten percent which was better than what they were paying. Our accountant was adamant we shouldn't because that kind of rescue just leads to more credit card debt. So again, no. And that was it, they cut themselves off from us completely. Never heard a word from them. I wasn't too upset. But Mary, well she suffered." Michael turned to his wife.

"I missed my grandchildren."

Father Gilbert nodded his understanding.

"So that was that until one day I had a serious accident. Could've killed me and I was laid up on the couch and Mary let the family know and my son turned up to see me. We had a good talk and he invited me to his house to have a talk about things. We even arranged a mediator. My daughter-in-law was good enough to agree but we knew she was carrying a lot of hurt and we wanted someone else there to guide us through. They say anger hides a lot of hurt. My daughter-in-law went first and she had obviously been very badly hurt. I interrupted at one stage and corrected her on a few things because we were being made to look pretty bad in front of that mediator.

"Mary wanted so badly to be in touch with the grandchildren she didn't try and defend us. She just said she was sorry we had caused upset but that she had done the best she could. And that was fine, but I couldn't do that. I listed all the things we had done. The money we *had* given them. Having them stay in our home for about eight months while they couldn't get a house. And all the rest of it. I wasn't at my best, Father. She would have to be a very holy person to have anything more to do with me anymore. But the good news was that after that meeting, they agreed for Mary to go on outings with the children.

"So, every week I would drive Mary to some rendezvous ahead of the pre-arranged time and then go off and make myself scarce. It worked well until one day, Mary received a long text from our daughter-in-law explaining she was going back home to Hong Kong with the children to stay with friends and, since my son didn't have a job there, he was going to stay here until he did. Tell Father what happened, Mary."

"I just said 'OK, thanks.' Her explanation for going back to Hong Kong was very long. She had never been happy here in New Zealand. I think she rightly read things into my short response and I haven't been able to visit with the children since. I've tried but all my texts are ignored. Fortunately, Covid put an end to her going back to Hong Kong."

Hoping his wife would say more and seeing she

wasn't prepared to, Michael resumed their story, "So we were sent to Coventry until . . ." Michael paused. He was smiling. "Until my granddaughter started playing soccer and my son couldn't resist letting me know how she was going. I asked if we could come and watch her, and he agreed on the condition we made ourselves scarce. And we did. My granddaughter was a natural and I offered to give her five dollars a goal. She was scoring lots of goals.

"Anyway, one day I told my son I would bring the money I owed my granddaughter and he was good with that. So we turned up and stood on the sideline opposite to them, as usual, and all went well until after the game when I waved the envelope with the money over my head to get my granddaughter's attention. She came over to get it and we had a little chat and off she went. A few hours later, I received an abusive text from them telling me I had engineered the whole situation to be able to make contact with my daughter-in-law."

Michael closed his eyes and let out a big sigh. "That was it for me. I told Mary enough was enough."

Father Gilbert looked to Mary whose eyes were averted.

There was a long silence. Michael let out another sigh. "I'd had enough." He looked to Mary but she wouldn't be drawn. "I should say that no matter how they treated us Mary has continued be loving and kind, sending them gifts, sending them texts. She never gives up, but this time I asked her to call it quits. I just couldn't stand seeing the anguish she was going through." He paused and looked to Mary for support and she gave a quick nod.

"I have to be honest here, Father, and this is why I

felt such a fraud at the meeting with those young couples. I told Mary that I could not put up with her continually chasing after them and that if she didn't agree to call it quits then we would have to live separate lives. I mean it's scriptural isn't it, Father, 'Don't throw your pearl before swine.'"

Father Gilbert said nothing, then slowly nodded his head and Michael understood he was considering everything that had been said. The Finnertys, used to his considered approach, waited.

"So difficult," he eventually said, "so difficult. I understand. Show me a family these days where there is complete unity and harmony and I'll be surprised. It's everywhere. Even in my own family." He reached for the teapot.

"Oh no, Father," said Mary, "that'll be cold." She grabbed the teapot and went to the kitchen.

"Don't throw your pearl before swine," repeated Father Gilbert and raised his eyebrows. "Mmmm. I can understand that. I really can. Did I ever tell you I have a sister at the university? She's a lecturer. Married to the head of the philosophy department. A brilliant man. They met when my sister was one of his students. He's an atheist and my sister now calls herself an agnostic."

He stopped and smiled. "You know you can love people from a distance, Michael. Keep that distance but keep your heart open to them."

The fresh pot of tea had arrived and Father Gilbert poured himself a cup.

"Your sister," Michael prompted.

"Oh, yes. Actually, it's her husband I wanted to tell

you about. He can be aggressive in arguing his position. I think my being a priest is like a red flag to a bull. It gets tiresome. I've been banned from sending Christmas cards with nativity scenes. Oh, and banned from talking religion to his two children. My Catholic hocus pocus he calls it. Every time I make contact with them, I come away hurt and really question the point of maintaining contact."

"But you still keep seeing them?"

"Mmm," said Father Gilbert, "I do. I do."

"Does any good come out of that, Father?" asked Michael.

"Sometimes I wonder. Hard being a punching bag sometimes. But yes, I like to think so, though there have been times when I've given up on it. Loving them from a distance I call it."

"But you keep going back to them?"

"I do. Yes, I do." Father Gilbert looked at his watch. "Look I really must be going," he said and creaked his way into a standing position.

Mary ducked away into the kitchen and caught up with him at the front door. "Mustn't forget your banana cake, Father," she said and as he was leaving Michael invited he and Father Ward to dinner the following day.

Father Ward graciously declined the invitation. Going out to dinner with parishioners was not something he did. It was part of well thought out a course of action he called his '*modus operandi*'. Maintaining a professional boundary did not, in his considered opinion, allow for it. He was after all their priest, *in persona Christi.* It would not be appropriate to carry on like a friend and risk appearing vulnerable, talking about his fears and dreams. No, he needed to be someone apart, someone to whom they could come with their deepest concerns.

Father Gilbert, seeing his fellow priest was busy working on his sermon, did not pursue the matter. That particular conversation could wait for another day he decided and set about preparing his evening meal.

Chapter Eight

The Gospel for that Sunday was Mark's account of the Lord's cure of a demoniac in Capernaum. 'They went as far as Capernaum, and, at once, on the Sabbath he went into the synagogue and began to teach. And his teaching made a deep impression on them because, unlike the scribes, he taught with authority.

'In their synagogue there was a man with an unclean spirit and he shouted, "What do you want with us, Jesus of Nazareth? Have you come to destroy us? I know who you are: the Holy One of God." But Jesus rebuked it saying, "Be quiet! Come out of him!" And the unclean spirit threw the man into convulsions and with a loud cry came out of him.'

Father Ward was almost apologetic for the morning's Gospel, at pains to point out that possession by demons was extremely rare and they could be thankful they lived in a more enlightened age. "Conditions like epilepsy and schizophrenia," he said "now explain what once were labeled possession by some devil.

"I am reminded of an incident in my previous parish. A young woman was involved in a serious motor vehicle accident. She sustained head injuries and was confined to a wheelchair and a fundamentalist claimed she had been possessed. I was very angry that this fundamentalist would think such a thing and then burden this young woman with his ridiculous idea. She was very upset by it. On top of all the other suffering, she had she now had to contend with the idea her injuries were caused by some form of possession." Father Ward shook his head.

"My dear people, it is not in anybody's best interest to be looking for evil and make such pronouncements. Let us turn our thoughts instead to love, for where love is evil cannot flourish. With this in mind, I want to draw your attention to Our Holy Father's latest encyclical in which he calls for greater compassion towards refugees and asylum seekers and repeats his call for solidarity with the poor. And here I want to thank all those who are contributing groceries to our foodbank for the poor within our community. For where love is evil cannot flourish."

Father Gilbert, who was concelebrating the Mass, gave no hint of his reaction. That came later when he returned from his meal with the Finnertys. Father Ward was in the lounge attempting to de-stress, listening to Beethoven's Pastoral Symphony. He had paid a price preaching a sermon with a viewpoint no doubt at odds with Father Gilbert's. He was grateful Father Gilbert had been out for most of the day.

The older priest came loudly into the lounge full of good cheer, singing the praises of Mary's cooking. "You missed an excellent meal, Ian," he declared and Father Ward, conceding the inevitability of an early conclusion to Beethoven's symphony, turned the music off.

"Do you always decline these dinner invitations, Ian?"

"Yes I do," said Father Ward.

Father Gilbert asked why.

"It's just not something I do. I prefer my own cooking," said Father Ward.

"Really? Mary's a good cook."

This was not the conversation Father Ward had anticipated. It was almost a let-off and he was happy to have it. "It's part of my *modus operandi* I suppose you could say."

"Makes for a lonely life," said Father Gilbert, pushing back the recliner chair into which he had seated himself and lacing his hands behind his head.

"I have other priests with whom I can form friendships," said Father Ward, taking umbrage at the reference to loneliness. "My father was always in a leadership position. He used to say it was lonely but necessary."

Father Gilbert was suddenly serious and brought his chair into an upright position. The Finnertys had been hurt by Father Ward's refusal to accept their invitation and he believed the young priest was poorer for not having gone. "With all due respect to your dad, I disagree on this one, Ian. The best pastors I have known allow themselves to be part of the families in their parish. They celebrate their birthdays with them. They go on outings with them. They have meals with them."

"So, they relate to them as their friends as well as their parishioners?" asked Father Ward.

"Depends on what you mean by friends."

"Someone you can share your struggles with. Be

completely yourself."

"Not to that extent. There's always a degree of reserve. People understand that. They want that in their confessor. But a shepherd can smell like his sheep, without being one of them. He can get involved in their lives and show God's love."

"When you put it in those terms, it's hard to argue against," said Father Ward, smiling. He was willing to concede at least in theory and it was certainly a welcome reprieve from the conversation he thought he would be having.

"It's left only to God and angels to be lookers on," said Father Gilbert. "Francis Bacon."

"Yes, I've read that. A good point," he said casually and took up his remote in a pointed gesture to signal the conversation was finished. But Father Gilbert did not respond to innuendo. He was blunt and to the point and expected the same from others.

"I wanted to talk to you about that sermon of yours," he said looking at the remote. "I find it interesting that you should use the case of the demoniac at Capernaum to explain away cases of possession," he said.

"You disagree that a culture of love is more important than focus on devils?" asked Father Ward who could see he was not going to be spared this conversation but was more than ready.

"Not at all. 'Perfect love drives out all fear.' And fear as we know is the devil's tool. I just find it odd that someone who has called for the assistance of an exorcist would treat such an obvious case of possession in the Gospel as though it had no bearing on what's happening here in your own parish."

"Well, strange you should say that because I was approached by Mrs Alexander after Mass. She reports her son is no longer causing trouble. 'He's quiet and doesn't lose his temper anymore.' Her words. It seems we may have made an incorrect diagnosis. The fits of temper may well be just part of a phase he was passing through. Her words again. 'Just a phase he was going through.' She seemed embarrassed to see you were still here."

Father Gilbert considered this. It was not unusual for an evil presence to lie low and temporarily stop manifesting. He did not ask for the new explanation of the boy's facility in Latin. "Was the boy at Mass?" he asked.

"No."

"Is he showing any interest in saying the rosary or any other devotional practices?"

"No. But he is not being disruptive. He simply goes out of the house and walks."

"Interesting," said Father Gilbert, "we'll wait and see, shall we?"

There was a long silence.

Father Ward disagreed but was at a loss to find a polite way of saying so. In the end, it was Father Gilbert who broke the silence. "One of my heroes is Pope Leo the thirteenth. Are you familiar with his letters and encyclicals?"

Father Ward shrugged his shoulders. "Not really."

"In his opening remarks for *Humanum Genus* he makes the point there are two kingdoms and all men belong to one or the other. The kingdom of God and the kingdom of Satan. The church belongs to God's kingdom. It defends and promotes truth and virtue and is opposed to Satan and all his lies. That there is no devil is one of his lies."

Father Ward's impatience showed, but Father Gilbert seemed oblivious.

"No judgment, no punishment; no need to strive for virtue and no need for the grace of God's sacraments or obedience to His commands are other lies. I believe we have a duty, Father Ward to mention the devil from time to time because, believe you me, he hasn't gone away. Not from this world and, I strongly suspect, not from the Alexanders."

Father Ward said nothing. He simply nodded and reached for a book.

Father Gilbert retired early to his room that night and left Father Ward in the lounge reading. If Father Ward had quizzed himself on what he had read while Father Gilbert was still taking his recreation there he would have been unable to recall much of anything. With Father Gilbert gone, he ended the pretence and closed the book.

'We'll wait and see shall we?' Father Gilbert's words repeated in his mind. Wait and see. And how long was that going to take? It was not easy accommodating another priest in a small presbytery. Fortunately, Father Gilbert had seen the sense in accepting his gift of headphones and he no longer had to contend with Radio New Zealand's concert programme sounding loudly throughout the house. There was, however, no changing Father Gilbert's insistence on cooking his own dinner, a simple stew to which he added more water each night. Father Ward, who prided himself on his cuisine, took this as a slight.

The very presence of another priest in the small house, someone with views quite at variance with his own also carried with it a certain tension. It was not in Father

Ward's nature to disagree. To assert his own point of view was an ordeal and he would prefer to be free of having to do so.

He regretted asking the bishop for assistance. The hot, humid days of February moved slowly on and Father Gilbert's unhurried, casual attitude to the Alexander problem gave little hope of Father Ward reclaiming the freedom of living alone any time soon.

Father Gilbert continued with daily Masses and took heart from the gradual increase in numbers. He was not insensitive to Father Ward's need for time alone and continued walking down to the town after his breakfast each morning where he sat on a seat outside a cafe and took his time over a cup of coffee. He was becoming something of an identity, the old priest enjoying a coffee, happy to chat with anyone who had the time.

One of those people happened to be Michael. He took a seat beside Father Gilbert and explained he was waiting for Mary. "I wanted to thank you for what you said the other day. I'm back in touch with my son."

"Are you?"

"Yes, it was after you left. He texted me and asked if I would look after his dogs. They have a new rental which doesn't allow them. I couldn't believe the cheek of him after saying he regretted not knocking my block off. Long and the short is I texted back and told him he needed to apologise and he did and I'm looking after the dogs. I was so tempted to ignore his text but I thought a lot about what you said, Father. How you just kept going with that brother-in-law of yours. And it came to me I wasn't doing the right thing because I felt uneasy about it and kept having to justify it to myself."

"Good for you."

Michael snorted and shook his head. "I even brought him a ticket to come with me to watch the Black Caps in Auckland and said I'd take care of accommodation. He texted back that he wanted to take his family with him and I asked what's wrong with a man taking a weekend off from family. Well that led to the usual. Who am I to be telling him how to run his family. The usual run of disrespectful stuff. He said he didn't want to go without his family. I don't have to guess to know who was behind that." Michael sighed.

Father Gilbert nodded his understanding. "Some relationships are just there to try us. A cross. But I think you were right to be in contact. I always think of Peter trying to protect Jesus from the cross. They were on their way to Jerusalem and He told them of the suffering he would have to endure and Peter said no way, that's not happening and Jesus said 'Get behind me, Satan.' The Lord recognised it for what it was. The devil hates it when we accept a cross."

Before Michael could respond to this, Mary arrived. She was beaming and had a shopping bag full of gifts for her grandchildren and they took their leave, with Michael simply giving the priest a nod and a smile.

Dean Collins had taken to coming into town several times a week. An old familiar restlessness was stirring within Dean, and he was looking for something to break the monotony of life at the beach. It was easy enough getting a ride into town. The locals in the beach community had come to know him and, if he was on the road as they left for work, they were happy to give him a lift.

Trying to remember where he had seen Father

Gilbert before had exercised his mind for days until the urgency of it faded and he surrendered to the incapacity of an alcohol-addled brain. But that morning, when he came out of the chemist with a prescription for valium, he had convinced one of the doctors he needed, he looked across the street, saw Father Gilbert and knew straight away where he had seen him before. He stood stock-still in amazement at what his memory had just served up.

"You alright, mate?"

"Yeah, yeah," said Dean, realising he was standing in the middle of the footpath, staring across the road with a dumbstruck look on his face. He collected himself and sat down on a nearby seat, without taking his eyes off Father Gilbert. "Bloody hell, it's him alright." The man had aged well. A full head of hair and that same smooth Mediterranean complexion. But it was the way he cocked his head and gave a half smile, that same friendly open manner that gave him away. And his name? His name? That still eluded Dean. But it didn't matter. He knew him. Knew he wasn't no priest. But there he was acting like one.

Dean averted his eyes. Didn't pay to let him know he was on to him. Not just yet anyway. He needed to know more. He glanced back and kept Father Gilbert in the corner of his eye. His mind was racing. If he was playing the part of a priest up there at the Catholic church, then this little discovery could be worth something. He followed Father Gilbert up to the presbytery, watched him disappear inside and almost rubbed his hands with glee. Only the presence of the other priest stalled Dean from confronting Father Gilbert there and then. He would find out the time for Masses and return the next morning, in the hope of catching the 'imposter' alone.

Father Gilbert was more than surprised to see Dean Collins in the pews. He was disturbed. Dean was an unpleasant individual. Manipulative and dishonest, he could be troublesome. He deliberately prolonged his time in the sacristy, in an effort to avoid him, but Dean was not that easily put off. He was there to greet him as soon as he emerged, a sly grin on his face. "Remember me?"

"Yes, I remember you, Dean," said Father Gilbert.

Dean folded his arms and stood back taking Father Gilbert in, grinning at the frayed look of his clericals. "You been doing this a long time."

"Doing what?"

Dean laughed. "I know who you are. I remember yous. We used to get drunk together. Remember? Course you do. You was a rum man. And me with me Old Pale Gold. I could never afford rum. But you had a job. You was a painter. See, I don't forget nuffink." He paused, nodding his head in admiration. "You said that Mass good, too. Like you were the real deal." Good enough, in that he had no clue what he was saying, usually an indication to him someone was smart.

"Is there something I can do for you, Dean?"

"For me? It's more what I kind do for you, mate."

Father Gilbert took a big breath, struggling to keep his patience. "Dean, I have things to do."

"What kind of things?"

Father Gilbert folded his arms.

"That other priest he don't know does he? Course he don't. But don't worry 'cause yuh secret is safe with me, mate. I wouldn't want to spoil things for yuh, would I?

'Course if I'm gunna do yous a favour, then it's only right that ah . . . well, you know. Fair's fair."

"You want some money?" asked Father Gilbert.

"That'd be good. Doesn't have to be a lot."

"I see," said Father Gilbert. "Blackmail."

Dean put up his hands. "No, no, no," he said, offended by the suggestion. "No. Just something for an old mate to keep things on the hush-hush."

"Okay, Dean, let's get a few things straight, shall we? First of all, I'm not your old mate. You stole from me and every other man you found sleeping rough. Secondly, I don't care who you tell about my past life. It may surprise you to know I was a priest before you met me and I'm a priest again now."

"No you ain't," said Dean. "You was always a smooth talker for a painter but you never fooled me. Just another alkie like the rest of us. And you don't fool me now, mate." Dean's tone had changed, there was an edge to it now.

Father Gilbert moved to the door of the church and held it, waiting for Dean to leave.

"You're making a big mistake, mate. This little game of yours will be all over with just one word from me. I could go up there right now and tell that real priest what yous are up to."

"Go right ahead, Dean," said Father Gilbert nodding towards the presbytery door.

"No. No. I can see you're upset and not thinking straight. You don't want to be throwing away a roof over your head and your share of all that money they put on the plate. Do yuh? Tell yuh what I'll do for yous. I'll give yous a day to think about it. Only a day. And if you haven't got some dorayme for me by then, I'm spilling the beans."

Father Gilbert walked up the stairs towards the presbytery without another word. "I'll do it, mate," called Dean after him. "Sure as my name is Deano Collins."

The next day, Father Gilbert did not take his usual walk. He drove out to the coast. A snakeskin sea crawled to the shore and broke in small waves. He remembered a line from a novel: shark infested waters breaking on an unfriendly isle, peopled by hostile natives.

The sun went in behind a lowering sky moving over the bay as he stepped from the car. A rickety handrail gave way as he went down some steps to the beach. All his weight was momentarily carried by his gammy leg. The pain took his breath away. He hobbled to a log, washed up from the sea and sat down to rest, stretching out his leg in front of him. The pain suddenly stopped, like walking out of gale force wind into the lee side of a building and he sat in a daydream enjoying the reprieve. After a long while, he told himself he should really be back at the presbytery helping Father Ward, but lingered on, enjoying the pleasure of daydreaming when work was calling.

A freak wave carried right up the shore and he lifted his shoes from the wash. He stood and wondered when Dean Collins would come calling. For come calling he would. There was no doubt in Father Gilbert's mind about that. He paused at the top of the steps and looked at the serried ranks of waves crawling relentlessly toward an unyielding shore.

Beyond the bay, the heave of the ocean threw up whitecaps. Ceaseless, vast and seemingly without bounds, the ocean was not what it seemed. Bound by space and time, it was not endless. There was something in that thought, but the ache in his leg was back and the pleasure of philosophising was gone. It was time to head back to town and whatever awaited.

By lunch time, realising he wasn't going to show, Dean made his way up from the town to the presbytery. He could see the other priest was at home with the 'imposter' and decided to wait, out of sight. He settled down for the vigil in some bushes, close to the priests' house. In this he was well prepared, having bought with him his weekly groceries and a flagon of Old Pale Gold. Setting up camp in shadowed, out-of-the-way places was nothing new to him. But as luck would have it he didn't have to wait long. A few minutes later Father Ward left in his car. Dean immediately left his hiding place and went up to the presbytery door. Father Gilbert opened after the first knock.

"Hiding from me was yous?" asked Dean.

"Dean, if this is about what you mentioned yesterday, then you go right ahead and do whatever it is you have in mind. There's no money here for you, Dean." He closed the door.

Dean banged loudly on the door until Father Gilbert returned. "Yuh making a big mistake," said Dean.

"There's no money here for you, Dean," repeated Father Gilbert.

"Right," shouted Dean, leaning in closely, his eyes blazing and his nostrils flaring. "I bloody warned yuh! It's on you now, mate. Say goodbye to the sweet life, yuh upperty bastard."

Chapter Nine

A few days later, Father Ward received a visit at the presbytery from Mrs Alexander. He had just returned from making his first visitation. A young family whose daughter had been withdrawn from the school. He was feeling very pleased with the outcome and keen to share with Father Gilbert, but Mrs Alexander's visit soon overshadowed that. She was in an agitated state and would not enter the presbytery until she was assured Father Gilbert was absent. The problem of her son had been set aside. She was back in her old role of policing improprieties.

Mrs Alexander was astute enough to preface her remarks with a word of caution about the reliability of her source. "I heard this from Jenny Walters whose husband heard it at the pub. And you know what they say about pub talk, Father. However," she said, taking a big breath, as she sat on the edge of her chair in the priest's lounge, gripping firmly the clasp of her handbag, "this is something so, so bizarre, I wonder if there might be some truth in it. They do say that truth is stranger than fiction and why would anyone come up with a story like this one."

Father Ward looked at his watch, a hint Mrs Alexander took umbrage at and launched into all Jenny Walters had passed on from her husband about Father Gilbert.

The absurdity of what was alleged inclined Father Ward to simply dismiss the gossip as nonsense. Sensing this, Mrs Alexander said, "I must insist on you confronting Father

Gilbert about these allegations. They must have some basis."

"Mrs Alexander, really, this is a respected priest."

"Then he has nothing to fear. I really must insist, otherwise I shall be taking my concerns to the bishop himself."

"That won't be necessary, Mrs Alexander. I shall certainly bring the matter up with Father Gilbert just to clear the air," said Father Ward and changed the topic with inquiries about her son which seemed to embarrass Mrs Alexander who now regarded that matter as something time had resolved.

That night when Father Ward spoke about her visit and her allegations Father Gilbert seemed bemused. "Shocking, isn't it?"

"Yes," said Father Ward, "I almost lost my patience. I'm not sure who on earth would put out a word as preposterous as that. Extraordinary."

"No," said Father Gilbert, "I mean a priest sleeping under Grafton Bridge with the down-and-outs. Shocking."

Father Ward took pause.

"She was right in what she said. I have slept under Grafton Bridge with the down-and-outs."

Father Ward opened his mouth to speak but thought better of it. He tried to read what was behind his fellow priest's words. He was looking for a lead, a laugh, a quick dismissal of what had just been said. Then he had a slowly dawning revelation. "Oh," he said, an outreach, "you were doing missionary work among the down-and-outs. Living as they do."

"No," said Father Gilbert and let that take hold.

Father Ward was still at a loss.

"I was a down-and-out myself, Ian. An alcoholic. Grafton Bridge was a good last resort between rentals."

Father Ward could not respond to this for a long moment and then he said, "But you're a priest."

"Not then I wasn't."

"This was before you became a priest?" asked Father Ward still wrestling with the revelation, trying to make it fit.

"No, after I became a priest, though at the time I was no longer in the priesthood. Was working as a painter as a matter of fact."

Father Ward's reaction to all of this said more about his concept of the priesthood than any judgment he was making of Father Gilbert. This was extraordinary, momentous even. A priest, the diocesan exorcist no less, who had lived under Grafton Bridge. An alcoholic.

Alcoholism among his fellow priests was not novel or even exceptional. There were plenty functioning alcoholics who still maintained their priesthood and no doubt some who had given up the priesthood but this was a man who had been an alcoholic with the down-and-outs and was a priest again.

Father Gilbert guessed rightly what he was thinking and told him so. "I know," he said, "it defies all we hold dear about the ideal of priesthood. That a man like me, a man who has fallen is a priest again. Goodness me, I even gave up the practice of the faith. Never even went to Mass. How could a man like me ever be worthy of the priesthood again? I know exactly what you must be thinking because I thought exactly the same. Though that of course was after I had found sobriety. My mother, God bless her, suggested I return to the priesthood and I couldn't believe she would even consider such a thing. She'd seen me in drunken, abusive states. She knew what I had done. All of it. No, I could never be a priest, ever again. I wasn't worthy."

"But you are," prompted Father Ward.

"Yes, I am. That hound of heaven, he kept tracking me, wouldn't leave me alone. I took up the practice of the faith again. I went to Mass. But He wanted more. It seemed beyond belief but God seemed to be calling me back. It's a long story. Enough to say, this Mrs Alexander has it right."

"How on earth did she find out?"

"There's a man in town spreading the word. His name is Dean Collins. He knows me from Grafton Bridge."

"He doesn't know you were a priest?" asked Father Ward.

"No one knew and no one would ever suspect. I fitted in well because by that time I was a drunk too. Went straight to the pub every night after work and when they closed, I went to the bottle shop. I never told anyone I was an ex-priest and no one asked."

Father Ward gave a slight smile. It was a struggle to mask what he was really feeling. To say he was flabbergasted would hardly do justice to his stunned reaction. But he was quick to recover and gracious enough to say, "Thank you for that. I appreciate you sharing it with me. It's quite a story."

"Mmm."

Father Ward opened his mouth to speak again and then, thinking better of it, he said nothing.

"You were going to say something?" asked Father Gilbert.

"Um." Father Ward laughed. "Just that feeling of

unworthiness. I can relate to that."

"Why?"

Father Gilbert's directness could be disarming and Father Ward laughed to cover himself. He was still not used to it. "Well, I mean, don't we all? To be *persona Christi*. After all . . ." It was enough said and Father Gilbert left it there.

He sensed Father's Ward's sense of unworthiness was deeply felt and certainly was not the generic sense of unworthiness all priests grappled with. Father Gilbert could see that. But there had been enough said for one night and he rightly saw the young priest would need to process that long before he could move on to his own sense of unworthiness.

Realising Father Gilbert had said all he was going to on the subject of unworthiness; Father Ward resumed his professional manner. "All of which leaves Mrs Alexander," he said. "What are we to do about her?"

"I'll take care of that," said Father Gilbert.

The following Sunday, having taken on the task of delivering the day's sermon, he made his way slowly down the steps of the altar to stand in front of the congregation and an altar boy came down beside him and placed a chair. He paused as he always did and passed over the congregation with a smile, taking a moment to stare down Mrs Alexander's frowning disapproval, and then he began with a reference to the first reading: "'He who keeps his tongue, keeps himself out of trouble.' How true. How true. Gossip and rumours and slander would be unknown if we all could but honour the wisdom of the Book of Proverbs." He sighed and paused.

"In the Book of Wisdom we read, 'Blessed is the man who does not blunder with his lips and need not suffer grief for sin.' And need not suffer grief. There's a lot in that. And need not suffer grief for sin. For sin.

"Recall the incident in the Gospel when a paralyzed man is brought to Jesus on a stretcher. The first thing our Blessed Lord does is forgive him his sins. Have you ever wondered how a paralyzed man could commit sin? Well, wonder no more.

"My dear people, the sins of the tongue are multitudinous and when our time comes and we are in purgatory suffering for those sins we will envy the man born mute. And let us not forget the grief we will suffer here in this life.

"So, why do we do it? Why do we gossip, spread rumours and slander? Why?

"Allow me to digress. Last time I preached, I asked one of the altar boys what he thought of my sermon. And do you know what he said? He said he already knew what I had preached on. Already knew it. I'd wasted my time."

When the laughter stopped, he raised his hand. "So let me be sure I'm not wasting my time this morning. Stand up anyone who has never passed on gossip, spread rumours or slandered another person."

No one stood. He turned to see if his altar boys were standing. They were still seated. Then he sat down on the seat beside him.

"We're all in this together," he said as he stood back up. "Even an old priest falls for this temptation. You know how it goes. I hear Jack is cheating on Audrey. Did you hear Marjorie has been sacked? Did you know the Smiths' boy was caught shoplifting?"

Father Gilbert stopped and threw out his hands. "And

I think we all recognise it for what it is. It's mean spirited. So why do we do it? Isn't it that old sin of pride again? Because when we pass on something that makes others look bad, we feel superior. Don't we? I mean goodness me we would never cheat, get the sack or have a child who shoplifted. Aren't we wonderful?

"And isn't it a good piece of gossip delicious? You won't believe this, we say, but I've just heard that . . . And our friend goes on full alert, cranes forward, eyes wide, ears open. We know something they don't. There's that feeling of superiority again. And isn't that feeling of anticipation as our friend waits for us to deliver like taking that big ice-cream in hand and leaning forward to take the first bite. The old gossip juices are really salivating, aren't they? And once we've taken that first bite, we can't help ourselves, we just have to keep going. Oh, we might try and protect the person we're gossiping about with, 'Just between you and me,' or 'I know I can trust you not to tell anyone else.' But who are we kidding? Then, when we're on our own again, we get the gossip low, like the ice-cream sugar low, because our conscience knows we have erred and it tells us.

"It's even harder to resist when the person you are gossiping about has hurt you, not someone else, but *you*. It's harder because you're hurting and you want comfort in your pain. Let's say, for instance, one of your adult children has said awful things to you about their childhood and the way you treated them. And I hear of this often because children get to an age when they look back critically on their childhood. If that's not you, and your children actually thank you for all you did for them, be grateful. But so often I hear, in this present age, adult children complain to their parents about their upbringing. And it hurts, especially when parents look back on all the sacrifices and hardships they endured to give their children the best they knew how at the time.

"The temptation to enlist the complaining child's siblings, to tell them what their brother or sister has said, is enormous. What are we looking for with that kind of gossip? Isn't it true that we want the other person to affirm us in our belief we're a good person. Aren't we looking for someone to say, 'You didn't deserve that, they should never have said that.' And isn't it also true we are looking for someone to join us in our strong negative feelings towards the person who hurt us. They hurt us and we want to hurt them. Remember when we were children and we'd say to someone who hurt us, 'I'm gunna get a gang onto you.'? Isn't that what we're trying to do here. Trying to turn others against someone who has hurt us. Trying to make sure they get their just deserts.

"But, my dear people, it doesn't work. We need to keep that kind of talk to ourselves. Keep it to ourselves! And be very watchful, for you are walking about with your own downfall. And here I'm quoting from The Book of Wisdom. You only make things worse. As the author says, later in the same book, 'be as one who knows and yet holds his tongue.'"

At that point in his sermon, Father Gilbert was suddenly interrupted by someone shouting out, "I know who you are." It was so unusual and unprecedented, like the clash of a symbol during a piano recital, the whole congregation turned as one to see who it was. Mrs Alexander's hand went up to her mouth. She sat rigid and unmoving, a world of turmoil in her eyes. Her husband stood, but Father Gilbert, who was moving towards the young man calling out, gestured for him to resume his seat.

"I know who you really are. Have you come to hurt me?"

Mark Alexander, who had been standing in the entrance to the nave of the church, backed into the foyer at Father Gilbert's approach, but then stood his ground, grinning at the priest, staring with an intensity of hatred those who saw it found unnerving. Father Gilbert raised his hand and prayed. "In the name of Jesus Christ, I bind you and command you to silence."

The effect was immediate. Mark hunched his shoulders and withdrew from the church like one who had been struck and those who saw it said Mark seemed to crumple and come to his senses as though he had been under some kind of spell. Father Gilbert returned to the foot of the altar and paused while the congregation recovered. Then he resumed his sermon as though nothing had happened.

"My dear people, gossip doesn't work, but there is something else that does." And here Father Gilbert turned to the crucifix behind the altar and gestured toward Christ on the cross. "Take your pain to Him. He understands. Imagine the temptation he must have had to justify himself to the apostles when all the Pharisees were saying unconscionable things against him? But there is not one Gospel reference to him giving in to that temptation. Take your pain to Him and He will comfort you.

"And let me finish with a story. A friend of mine, a teacher, was called in to the office of her principal where he proceeded to tell her of several unjust allegations about her teaching competency made by other teachers. My friend sat in silence, telling herself that God was her defender that she had done nothing wrong and He would look after her. Well, that principal went on and on in the face of her silence, until eventually he stopped and said, 'Of course, I don't really accept what they're saying. Your students love you. The parents are very pleased with their children's progress. I shouldn't really listen to what your colleagues have been saying.'

"My dear people, God has our back, trust Him. And remember, too, if people are saying bad things about you for no good reason, you're in good company. They treated the saints in exactly the same way. Saint Padre Pio was accused by other priests of being greedy and evil.

"Greedy and evil," repeated Father Gilbert and laughed. "Padre Pio. One of our greatest saints. And the local bishop believed the gossip. He believed it and Padre Pio was confined to his monastic cell for several years. He said not one word in his defence. God took care of that for Him. So my dear people, to conclude, be as one who knows yet holds his tongue."

Mr and Mrs Alexander did not stay for the final hymn and were well gone by the time Father Gilbert and Father Ward processed from the altar to the sacristy. But Father Gilbert was convinced it would not be long before they heard from them.

Mrs Alexander had endured quite a morning. As far as she was concerned, Father Gilbert's sermon had been directed at her and, initially, she had sat through it with a mounting fury only the self-righteous know. Mark's sudden interruption from the back of the church was like a bucket of cold water on that smouldering fire and her reaction was almost catatonic. Worse awaited her return to the farm where Mark sat waiting for them in his father's overheated farm truck, steam pouring from the bonnet.

Any thought Harry Alexander may have had of taking his son to task about his truck was immediately shelved when Mark came bearing down on them.

"Quickly, Harry, lock the doors," counselled Mrs Alexander and cringed. Whatever it was that possessed her son was out of hiding and back in full force. Only Mrs Alexander's pride prevented her from immediately phoning the presbytery for assistance. Kicking in the paneling of their car, Mark went on a rampage inside the house until he was utterly spent. Reviving enough to start a fire in the kitchen, he then roared down the road on the farm bike.

He returned late that night to find the house locked and all the lights out. His parents waited anxiously in the dark, fearing he might force his way in. Instead, he roared off down the road again and they were left to spend a sleepless night in dread of him returning. Mrs Alexander felt guilty for not being worried about her son's own well-being; she was too terrified for her own.

When they did not hear from him for several days and word came to them Mark was staying at his girlfriend's place, they breathed a sigh of relief. Mrs Alexander lit several candles in front of a statue of Our Lady in the hope the Blessed Mother would protect them. Her fervent prayers during the days that followed did not extend to the Gillespies, the parents of Bella, Mark's girlfriend. As far as she was concerned, the Gillespies were getting their just deserts. Rightly or wrongly, all blame for Mark's spiritual condition had been laid at the feet of the Gillespies and their promiscuous daughter.

Wanting to protect Mark from bad influences at the local school, Mrs Alexander had applied to the Ministry of Education for Mark to study with the Correspondence School. The application was successful.

Once a year, the Correspondence School organised camps. There, parents were able to network with others for mutual support. At one of these camps, Mrs Alexander made the acquaintance of Mrs Gillespie or Kezia as she liked to be known, not her real name, but one that suited her gypsy aspirations.

Kezia, with her sevillana dress, her bare feet, her large bangle earrings and her gypsy fortune teller's head scarf, certainly stood out. Her husband, Stefan, again not the name he had been christened with, also spurned shoes, and, with his wide leather belt, his corduroy trousers, his long-sleeved shirt and his gypsy vest also cultivated the look of a gypsy. They lived in two colourful caravans, drawn by two large Clydesdales horses, constructed in wood to resemble a Romany gypsy version. Kezia and Stefan had a daughter named Bella. She and Mark were only six at that first camp and Mrs Alexander saw their mutual friendship as harmless enough.

The Gillespies lived just down the road as it turned out and Mark was often invited to come and play with Bella, something Mrs Alexander had reservations about when Bella flowered into a bewitchingly, beautiful teenager. But that should have been the least of Mrs Alexander's concerns. The Gillespies' influence on Mark had gone far beyond any attraction he had for Bella. They were New Age advocates and Mark saw their lifestyle and values as far more appealing than his mother's dreary version of religion. They were "free spirits" who had no problem with "free love". They smoked a little pot, embraced a lifestyle closer to Nature, and used Eastern techniques to realise their higher selves.

But by the time Mark and Bella had become adolescents, the Gillespies had broken ranks with most New Age advocates and advanced their quest for a higher self beyond crystals, mantras and meditation. They were now using tarot cards, Ouija boards, séances, necromancy and channeling to help them gain 'their share of the universe's divine essence'. Mark was often invited to join them in their séances.

Mrs Alexander had worked hard to protect her son from the world's evil. She allowed no television in the house. The only phone she would allow was a landline. All digital devices like tablets and iPads were taboo. And she carefully monitored his selection of books at the local library.

By the time Mark was seventeen and sexually active with Bella, he had become very adept at maintaining his secret life, relying on Bella to supply him with condoms and a farm worker he had befriended to supply him with pornographic literature. But while he was cunning enough to keep his supply of pornography hidden in nearby bush, he was not so careful with his condoms. When his mother discovered them, she was horrified and banned all contact with Bella.

Eventually conceding that was a lost cause when she caught him sneaking away to the Gillespies during the day, she enrolled Mark at the local High School. Any negative influences at the school being viewed as the lesser of two evils, which is not to say she did not work hard to mitigate such negative influences, strictly enforcing a no-parties-or-girls rule. She even went so far as to ban Mark from bringing home some of the literature assigned by his liberal English teacher. Mark's father played his part by taking Mark to and from school, in case he was waylaid by the bewitching Bella.

Not to be outdone in any of this, Mark read *Portnoy's Complaint*, *Lady Chatterley's Lover* and *A Clockwork Orange* several times in the school library. He watched the film version of Anthony Burgess's A *Clockwork Orange* so many times on a friend's iPad, he could quote almost every scene word for word. And every weekend he found a way of meeting up with Bella.

Mark's interest in the devil had pre-dated the Gillespie's interest in the occult. Drawing pictures of Satan and demons had been a secret practice since he was fourteen. He took great pleasure in doing the one thing he knew his mother would abhor. When Mark heard his mother and her friends railing against the Masons, he was all ears. The idea there was an organisation where men in the higher levels actually worshipped Lucifer fascinated him and he went online at the school library to read everything he could. He was disappointed to learn the local Masonic lodge had closed years earlier but found other ways to make his stand against religion.

He took pride in calling himself an atheist and tried to enlist Bella in his anti-religious cause. Bella did not share his interest. But Mark, who was something of an obsessive, would not leave it alone and kept trying to engage her with whatever he learned. "Listen to this Bella, Karl Marx said, 'The criticism of religious doctrine concludes, for men, the Supreme Being is Man.'"

"Oh, Mark, do you have to talk about that stuff. It sounds like Mum's New Age bullshit."

"It's not. Karl Marx understood, Bella. Stalin was the same. 'Against the propagation of religious nonsense, the Communist Party can only continue the war.'"

Bella, who had introduced Mark to cannabis, was not pleased with the way it seemed to animate him in his proud boastful declaration of atheism. She preferred to indulge in sensual pleasures. The problem came to a head one day when Mark interrupted Bella's best attempts at seduction by breaking off to share something from his reading that morning: "Lenin writes, 'Faith in God is a monstrous cowardice.' Monstrous cowardice, Bella. My mother and her cronies are afraid to face up to the world as it is. There is no God, Bella."

Bella, while not nearly as intelligent or curious as her boyfriend, was shrewd enough to realise Mark's atheism implied a denial of all things spiritual. Her mother's dabbling in the occult was enough to convince Bella that wasn't true. There was a spiritual realm alright and, in an effort to shift Mark's thinking from what had evolved into the horribly boring ravings about the dialectical materialism of atheistic communism, she asked her mother's help. By that time, Kezia's dabblings in the occult had advanced to regular summonings of what she referred to as presences.

Mark soon realised the spirits Kezia was summoning were giving her knowledge she could easily have used to have influence over others. This appealed to Mark. While Kezia may have referred to these spirits as presences, Mark knew from all his mother had warned him about occult practices exactly what they were. It was the same devil and his demons he had been fixated with for years.

While Catholicism counselled humility, obedience and service of others, Satan offered power, rebellion and the cultivation of oneself into what the Masons called a Supreme Being. Mark was all for it and relished Mrs Gillespie's initiation into the occult.

Father Gilbert was not surprised at Mark's sudden return to Mass. He had been expecting it. If Mrs Alexander had told Father Ward of the rumours circulating about him it was almost a certainty she would have been speaking of them within Mark's hearing. Father Gilbert believed the demon would have gained confidence from what it perceived to be the priest's weakened position. In that, it had been mistaken. But Father Gilbert also knew the demon's anger at being publicly humiliated in a church would have repercussions far beyond anything the Alexanders could tolerate and he awaited their call.

Harry Alexander, though moderately religious himself, a matter of having to be, did not share his wife's belief in the power of prayer alone to protect them from their son; and one day, while in town collecting some fence posts, he called up to the presbytery. It was a Monday and Father Gilbert was there on his own.

Chapter Ten

Harry came straight to the point. "We're having trouble with the boy again, Father and I think we still might need your help." Not to be hurried in this, Father Gilbert invited Harry in and made a cup of tea.

"That farm of yours," said Father Gilbert pouring the tea, "dairy or beef?"

"Beef," said Harry taking the proffered cup of tea.

"Always been a farmer, Harry?"

"Oh, yes," said Harry, "born and raised on that farm. Farming's all I've ever known, Father."

"And your good wife?"

"No. She was a townie when I met her. We married late in life." He smiled. "Folk round here had me figured for a lifelong bachelor. Bit shy with the lady folk but then someone introduced me to Sandra. After Mass one Sunday it was. And it went from there."

"Very religious lady I understand."

"Oh yes, there's that about her alright. Me I'm just a practical, common sense kind of man with what you'd call a simple faith. Mass on Sunday. A morning offering to start my day. And an act of contrition and a prayer to my guardian angel at night. My Sandra, she's a bit more full on than that."

"In what way, Harry?"

"Well, she's a Mass-every-day kind of person. You know the rosary and prayers to the saints and goodness knows what else. But don't get me wrong, Father. I've always been okay with it. Sandra, she comes from a broken home and religion has always been a comfort to her."

Harry declined the offer of a biscuit. "Anyway, Father, about Mark."

"Yes, yes," said Father Gilbert sensing Harry's impatience. "Acting up, is he?"

Harry shook his head. "Worse than it's ever been."

"I see," said Father Gilbert, "tell me, Harry, has Mark

been okay with his mother's devotions."

Harry closed his eyes and cocked his head. "Well that's the thing. No, he hasn't. Was never going to be easy being the son of parents in their forties if you understand my meaning. Younger parents they're into more fun stuff, I think. And we knew that. But I think his Mum being very religious made it worse."

"In what way?"

"Well, Father, if faith is a gift, then I don't think my son ever had it. His Mum's best efforts made no difference. I could see he was never going to have it. But Sandra insisted he join her for the rosary every night right from when he was a little boy and you could see it was just a torment. Same thing repeated again and again. He hated it. Only got worse as he grew older. But Sandra she kept on.

"Then one day, I happened to be in the bush looking for a stray cow and I came across this carving in a tree. He was about fifteen at the time, I think. I didn't pay it much mind. I mean he was always one for doing sketches. But as I walked around in the bush, I kept seeing the same sketch. It was a star inside a circle."

"A pentagram?"

"Yeah that was it, a pentagram. Course I didn't know that at the time. Had to look it up."

"A symbol of Satanism," said Father Gilbert.

"Yes, that's what they reckon alright. Put the woollies up me to tell you the truth, Father. I should've done something about that. I just figured he probably didn't know what he was doing and put it in the too-hard-basket. I should've done something. Didn't even tell his mother.

"Mark has never been an easy boy. When my

parents, Mark's grandparents, were alive they said we were spoiling him. He was so wilful and stubborn, it was hard to discipline him and we often gave in. It was just easier. We like things quiet and peaceful, Sandra and me. When he became a teenager, he was very moody and best left to himself. We didn't ask much of him. I never involved him in work around the farm. It was just easier. Sandra was different. She gave so much of her time to him. She wanted to protect him from everything. Any chance of that was gone the day he made friends with the Gillespie girl down the road," said Harry and sighed.

"The Gillespies?" Father Gilbert wanted to know more.

"Hippies, I suppose you'd call them. Into that New Age stuff. We banned him from going down there, but he'd sneak out at night. Sandra was convinced they were into the occult because of what people were saying. You know how people talk in a small community. Anyway, one night we were woken at about two in the morning. It was Mark. He was in the kitchen looking for something to eat, making a terrible racket, cooking himself up something and his mother was fit to be tied. She raged out there, in her dressing gown to put him straight. Before she could say a word, Mark turned on her. There was a terrible ruction. I rushed out of bed to find the kitchen in a shambles. The fridge pushed over, table upended, fist holes in the walls. He had his mother pinned to a wall, both hands around her throat."

Harry closed his eyes in dread at the memory and took a big breath before continuing, "It was the look in his eyes, Father. It was . . . Not Mark. Put it that way. Cold and empty that look was. And he was grinning. Enjoying himself. I grabbed a frying pan and belted him over the back of the head. Knocked him unconscious. When he came to he seemed to be himself again. He looked around at the mess in the kitchen with confusion and went off to bed.

"His mother was in a terrible state. Neither of us slept a wink that night. I told her about the pentagrams and she told me something she'd been keeping to herself as well: a sketch book she found hidden in Mark's bedroom. It was full of sketches. Sketches of the devil. Sandra was convinced where the blame lay and I went down to the Gillespies the next morning. Young Bella locked herself in her caravan and wouldn't come out and I didn't get much sense from her parents either. They gave the impression they didn't know what on earth I was talking about. But when I looked back, Bella was standing at the window of her caravan watching me leave. She was crying.'

"We tried to put it behind us, but that was impossible. Living in the same house as Mark was a nightmare. You never knew when he was going to lose his temper. He was so violent. And he liked to taunt us. He mocked us when we were praying and whenever we went off to Mass. It got so we didn't want to live in our own home, but we daren't leave him to have the run of the place. We came back from Mass one Sunday and the dog was dead.

"Funny thing about that dog. From the moment Mark came home that night when it all started that dog started growling and whining. Same way he carries on when there's a rat in the house. He'd bark his head off whenever Mark went near him.

"We'd brought that dog for Mark when he was a little boy to keep him company. They'd grown up together.

Inseparable when they were younger. And he killed it. It was horrible. Had the poor creature strung from its hind quarters from a tree. I think he'd stabbed it with a pitchfork. There were three stab wounds like they'd come from the three tynes of a pitchfork.

"Another time we came back from Mass and some of Sandra's holy paintings were missing. Not the crosses. And not the statues. But some of the paintings. We found the remains of them in the incinerator. It was after that I cleaned out the batch the farm worker had when we had one and insisted Mark live down there. There was no fuss. He seemed to prefer it and it *was* better. Didn't stop his mother worrying though. She wanted to take Mark to a doctor. And one day he agreed to go to a doctor. Sometimes it was like we had our Mark back and whoever it was that he became when he went off wasn't there anymore. The doctor couldn't do anything for Mark. He referred us to psychological services. They tried to help, but they couldn't.

"They said he had more than one personality. Multiple Personality Disorder was the term they used. But when they tried to find a reason for it there was nothing we could tell them. There was no what they called trauma while he was growing up.

"One of them actually suggested we go to a priest. Made it easier to get help from Father Ward when we told him we'd been to a doctor and psychological services."

Father Gilbert nodded. "You say Mark can be violent on occasion and that he likes to taunt you, to mock you. Would you say the presence responsible for these behaviours was one and the same?"

Harry was a man of the land, a man who enjoyed his

own company, with the luxury of time to think any problem through, without any need to rush. He was slow and deliberate in his response to this question, recognising it for what it was: a difficult one. “Father, if we’re talking demons here then here’s what I think. At the start, there was just this violent one and I think the taunting was all part of it. It didn’t say much. But then another one seemed to be there.” He closed his eyes and blew air from his cheeks, as though what he had to share was a little too much. “This other one uses Latin and talks a lot. Now my wife she knows a bit of Latin. Not much, but enough to get by when she attends Mass in Latin, so she knew the language but it took a while to work out what this demon was saying. The voice is frightening. It sounds old and evil if a voice can sound evil. Hard to describe really, but it does put the hairs up on the back of your neck. Deep and throaty. I’m no expert, Father, but I’d say there’s at least two of them and this other one really puts the wind up you.”

Harry was not a man given to emotion, but sleepless nights and the events of recent days had taken their toll. He paused to collect himself and took out a handkerchief from his pocket to dab his eyes. “It’s not Mark talking, Father. Mark doesn’t know Latin. It’s not his voice.” He swallowed and wrestled with the emotion. “Father, my son really does need you. We let Mark know you were here to help him when you first arrived at the presbytery and things returned to normal in a way. These demons seemed to disappear and Mark was so tired. Just slept and slept. He’s lost so much weight. But they haven’t gone. They’re still there. And they’ve got Mark going back to Mass causing trouble again.” Harry swallowed hard, closed his eye and tears ran down his cheeks.

"Okay, Harry," said Father Gilbert, putting his hand on Harry's shoulder, "the Lord will take care of your son. These demons are not in charge. The Lord is."

Harry sniffed and apologised for the show of emotion.

"Perfectly understandable," said Father Gilbert, "Now, Harry, you said Sandra was able to work out what this demon was saying."

"Well it speaks slow so Sandra was able to write down some of it. She got in touch with the priest for the Latin Masses and he translated the words. Filthy stuff it was, Father. Stuff I could never repeat. Horrible, filthy stuff. Nothing anyone could repeat really."

"Harry, you said there's at least two. What did you mean by at least?"

"Well, who's to say. I'm no expert, Father. That's your department. Could be just one for all we know. Maybe it has different voices. There is another voice though. This one lies. It'll tell you things that aren't true."

"What sort of things, Harry?"

"Well things like: 'We're going. No need for a priest.' And this one it knows things about me and Sandra. Personal things. Things only Sandra and I should know. Like I say personal things. Embarrassing things. And he taunts us with these things. But he also adds lies, things that aren't true. Awful things. Things it says I've done behind Sandra's back. Things she's supposed to have said about me. Lies. But then it says these things that are true which no one else should know. It does my head in, Father. How would he know these things?"

Father Gilbert pursed his lips and cocked his head. "It's difficult to say. He may have been watching you. More likely, he's guessing. We must remember demons are fallen angels. They are highly intelligent and have been observing human beings since the dawn of time. They can guess a lot of things from the way a person presents, just on what they have observed over millennia. They can't read your thoughts but they can guess, probably on the basis of things like body language.

"Look, Harry, I'm here to help but from what you say I suspect your son has invited these demons in and that kind of entry point is more difficult to deal with. It may take some time is what I'm trying to say. But first, you'll need to share this conversation with your wife. I'll need both your permission *and* hers to proceed any further."

"All that horrible stuff one of those voices says about Sandra . . . It's embarrassing. She's a proud woman my wife. And then there's this gossip she's been hearing about you, Father."

"Well," said Father Gilbert, leading Harry to the door, "when you're both ready for Father Ward and I to come and perform the exorcism, you let me know. In the meantime, avoid engaging with these demons. As you say, they'll do your head in if you take them seriously. Ignore what they're saying and pray this simple pray: In the name of Jesus Christ, I bind you. That should help."

Harry seemed reluctant to leave.

"When you're both agreed you let us know," Father Gilbert repeated closing the door. "All the best, Harry. Take care."

Chapter Eleven

Father Ward returned from his weekly tramp tired and out of sorts. He and his fellow trampers had set out to climb to a local trig station and encountered rough weather. They were forced to concede defeat not far from the summit and had encountered strong winds and torrential rain as they battled their way back to their vehicles at the bottom of the track. He was saturated and went for a shower while Father Gilbert fried up the meat patties he had prepared in anticipation of his return. He combined them with fresh tomatoes, lettuce and fried onions and stacked it all between fresh buns for a very passable hamburger. The meal raised Father Ward's spirits and made him more receptive to all the details of another eventful Monday at the presbytery.

Father Gilbert kept Harry Alexander's visit till last. He had other things to share that would set a lighter tone. A man claiming to be Father's friend had called. His name was Gerard and he wanted a cup of coffee. "He led me to believe you were always good for a cup of coffee and a sandwich."

"Did he now?" said Father Ward.

"He was very keen to fill me in on the latest developments in what I understood was a long ongoing ordeal with dubious friends. It seems one of them has sneaked in and stolen his new sheets and replaced them with dirty ones. He takes good care to lock the house when he leaves but they find their way inside. Which means he will have to wash the sheets again because these 'friends' are very unclean.

"His neighbours' children are still ringing his

doorbell and running off. He can hear them laughing when he comes to the door. He also wanted you to know he is very close to solving the Hodge conjecture. And he wants you to know he has finished the other work he was doing and is looking for a five-hundred-page notebook, the kind they used to have in Oakley. With five hundred pages, he will have room to do two graphs per page together with equations and evaluations. One thousand, a fitting number for the new millennium, he said."

Father Ward nodded. "A very full report, Father."

"An interesting caller."

"Gerard studied math at university before he suffered a breakdown. If he's on about people stealing his sheets again he probably needs his medication adjusted. He's harmless enough. Comes to Mass on occasion. Turns up towards the end and enjoys the spread the ladies offer."

"I see," said Father Gilbert and wandered if Father Ward could also solve the puzzle of children being over at the school playing when it was long after school had closed for the day. "I didn't recognise any of them from those I've seen at the school."

"No?" said Father Ward, "Well, I think I know the children you mean. Their parents drop them off here when they go to the pub. I keep an eye on them. Give them something to eat. They're better off here than roaming the streets. We have an understanding. I've told them to respect the property and not leave any rubbish behind."

Father Gilbert smiled. He liked this young priest. He had plenty to contend with, here all alone in this parish, hours away from the nearest fellow priest: the annoying visitors, the eccentric parishioners and those who liked to take advantage.

He could well remember the excitement of his first sole charge parish, fresh from the seminary, all fired up with the idealism of a young priest eager to serve. And the reality of what he faced falling so far short of his expectations.

Lahore, Pakistan was a world away from this parish but the challenges to this young priest's idealism were here as well. Five Mass centres he serviced and at one place he was lucky if three people turned up. The Catholic primary school on the property may have given him a captive audience for one Mass a week; but when they filed up during the distribution of Holy Communion they could only receive a blessing because most of them had not made their first Holy Communion. Their parents wanted them at a Catholic school but most of them saw no point in coming regularly to Mass or enrolling their children in the sacramental programme. Father Ward offered the body, blood, soul and divinity of Jesus Christ, the prize and consolation of martyrs and saints, God's greatest gift and all these young parents wanted from him was the sacrament of baptism so their children could be enrolled in a good school and get a good education for a well-paid job.

They had lost the faith it seemed.

The faith was the preserve of migrant families and the elderly. Those born New Zealanders had been reduced to a remnant. What Father Ward had to offer was not appreciated, understood or required. Among New Zealanders, Father Ward's sacred priesthood had been reduced to child minding, compassion for the lost and lonely and comfort for those coming to the ends of their lives.

"A social worker could have dealt with most of what

I saw today in your absence, Father."

"Exactly," said Father Ward.

"Except for one thing. Harry Alexander called in today. Only a priest can help that family, Father Ward. Only a priest."

Father Ward nodded. It was not the first time he had heard the phrase, 'only a priest can.' "Only a priest is capable of transubstantiation, Ian. Only a priest can give extreme unction, Ian." His Uncle Matt, the priest, pressed home the list whenever they spoke of the priesthood. Only a priest. "Trouble with Mark?" he asked, coming back to Father Gilbert.

"Yes."

Thinking the call to return to the Alexanders' farm had finally come, Father Ward took a deep breath and sat upright. He was ready. Ready to stand his ground this time. There would be no cowering or running. He would take whatever was meted out. Courage is fear that has said its prayers he reminded himself. The Alexanders were giving him the chance to redeem himself and he was well motivated to take it. Only they weren't.

Father Gilbert explained and added, "But it's only a matter of time. Mrs Alexander will concede the need for us soon I imagine. In the meantime, we should fast and pray and prepare ourselves. With that in mind, I would like you to hear my confession, Ian. And I can hear yours. We must do everything we can to ensure we bring Christ's presence with us. *Persona Christi*, Father Ward, *persona Christi*, because Jesus is the exorcist and we have nothing to offer without Him."

"So you're sure we're dealing with possession?"

"It's a reasonable possibility," said Father Gilbert, "bearing in mind it's rare here in the Western world. Two thousand years of Christianity is a formidable defence, especially in a relatively affluent country like our own. A culture close to pagan roots with poverty makes it more likely."

"Poverty?"

"Poor people are desperate people. They're willing to try anything."

"But you're reasonably sure it's a possibility in this case?"

"Mmm. And if I'm right, it'll be difficult because this young man, from what I can gather, invited them in."

"Them?"

"Yes, I think we may be up against more than one."

The memory of what Father Ward had encountered last time crowded in on his thoughts and he slumped back in his chair to collect himself.

"There's one other thing, Father. I'm pleased it has taken several weeks for this call to come. It's important you know the person you're working with. Demons work on our imaginations and our memories. They'll try to distract us with various physical manifestations and failing that, will taunt us, try to embarrass us. I know from what I have observed you are a good priest. Compassionate, kind and committed to your calling. But I also need to know of any secrets. Anything from your past life these unclean spirits could say to throw us off. Do you understand?"

Father Ward nodded gravely.

Dean Collins had pre-empted some of what Father Gilbert intended sharing with Father Ward about his own personal life. But not the worst of it. And it was his intention to share his entire story when he returned from his walk down the town the next morning. Father Ward spent a sleepless night considering what he needed to share and was grateful when circumstances intervened to temporarily put that daunting task to the side.

Chapter Twelve

The wife of one of the husbands seeking an annulment had called in to the presbytery in Father Gilbert's absence. She was distraught. Her husband was still resolved to seek an annulment and was planning on moving out of the home. "I've just dropped the children off at school," she said between sobs. "I haven't told them." She stopped and was convulsed by more tears.

Father Ward handed her a box of tissues and she regained her composure. "They were so happy when they knew we were both coming to the presbytery for counselling. Anthony, that's my eldest, said his prayers must be working. I just don't know what to tell them."

After expressing his sympathy and offering to continue praying, Father Ward's compassion rendered him silent and he saw her to the door, overcome by a feeling of powerlessness and inadequacy. He hadn't told her but he had seen her husband and the other woman in town. The other woman, a *femme fatale* if ever he had seen one, was younger, more attractive and seemed full of fun. The mother of his children could never compete in terms of looks and personality. Her youthful figure had been sacrificed in bearing his children and she seemed to know nothing of make-up, hairdressers or stylish clothing. She reminded Father Ward of a Swiss milk maid on a brochure advertising Switzerland. Plump, red-cheeked and dowdy. This husband of hers was trading up to a better model and Father Ward felt the injustice of it keenly.

Injustices occupied Father Ward's mind often. He was a collector of them and adding this new one to the list resurrected all the anger and indignation he felt every time. Unfortunately for Father Gilbert, he returned in time to bear the brunt of it. On and on he went about the inviolability of marriage, the sacredness of the contract and the suffering this husband was inflicting upon his wife and children.

"Good fuel for a sermon, Ian," was Father Gilbert's response and they retired to the lounge for their usual morning tea. "Saint Columba, was a man of your ilk, Ian." He smiled with fondness. "A rough character was our Columba. Swore like a trooper apparently but he was strong on marriage. His biographer tells the story of a woman who came to him in confession. She could no longer stand her husband and refused to sleep with him. Columba prayed for her and sent her away. But it did no good and she was back saying she loathed the man and could no longer share the marriage bed. So he asked her to come with her husband.

"In front of her husband, Columba told her that in denying him she was denying her own body because, as Scripture says, husband and wife are 'one flesh' He also suggested they join in prayer and fasting through the rest of the day, which they did. Only, after they had gone, Columba continued throughout the night, without going to bed. The next day, the woman declared the man she had hated was now the man she loved, that she had been changed during the night for reasons she did not know."

Father Ward drew small consolation from this.

"There's still the other couple to pray for, Ian," said Father Gilbert.

Father Ward nodded and the two men fell silent. Both priests knew this was the acceptable time to share whatever secrets they both had and they both felt the tension in the room. "Well, Father," said Father Ward clearing his throat, "I suppose now would be a good time to share anything. I'm not sure I'd characterise anything I want to say as a secret. I'm sure little I say will surprise you." His heart was thumping and he took a steadying breath and took a sip of coffee.

"Let me start, Ian, I'm happy to share first," Father Gilbert offered.

"No. I'm good to go. Just a moment." He stood up and went to the bathroom and as he came back into the room, he said, taking his chair, "The first thing is, I don't have much patience with these parishioners of mine from time to time. I actually refuse to answer the door, as you experienced, and I set my phone on silent and sometimes even delete messages without listening to them. I know it's bad but I've learnt if it's serious they'll see me at Mass." He smiled and took a sip of his coffee.

"Trivial I suppose but I've been wanting to say that since you arrived." He closed his eyes a moment, allowing Father Gilbert the chance to react and crossed his arms.

"Oh," said Father Gilbert, "you've just reminded me. Another visitor I had while you away on Monday. A huge fellow."

"Maori?" asked Father Ward, intrigued.

"Yes, he was as a matter of fact. Said he had re-enrolled his daughter at the school."

"Did he?" Father Ward was taken aback.

"Yes. Seemed pleased with himself."

"Not sure how he's going to afford that. I went out to visit the family last week. I'd noticed his daughter absent from class. One of those wonderful kids that wants to answer every question. A bright kid. Very challenging questions too. I missed her. When the principal told me the family had withdrawn her I just took it as one of those things but . . . Well truth be known, after you talked about getting more involved I thought I'd make that family my first visitation. Anyway, they invited me to lunch." He smiled. "Sausages and chips and fried bread. He's a very keen hunter. Hunts the same places I've tramped. We had a good talk. I told him how much I was impressed by his daughter. Seems they just couldn't afford the fees. I told him I would see what I could do. But you're telling me she's back."

"That's what he said."

"They'll be struggling. I'm pleased you told me. I'll look into that."

This exchange was to good effect and Father Ward seemed a little more relaxed when he went back to what he wanted to share. "My father was a hard man, Father Gilbert. He was a foreman down at the wharves." He laughed. "Dad was the stereotypical Kiwi male of a bygone era. Rugby, racing and beer. Murray Ball's Wal Footrot from Footrot Flats was my dad. He even got around in a black t-shirt. Big hands, big features, big beer stomach, almost the spitting image of Wal Footrot.

"I was the only child. They had me late. A very stressful pregnancy, I'm told. Anyway, out I came and I wasn't a future All Black, that's for sure. I was a big disappointment to my father. I tried. But it just wasn't in me to be the son he wanted. They always played me on the wing in rugby. Wouldn't have played me at all if Dad hadn't been such a legend, on the field, in his day He'd take me to rugby on winter mornings and I'd stand close to the sideline, holding my collar, shut against the cold, hoping the coach would take me off.

"I've always been somewhat effeminate in my manner. It was alright at primary. But different at high school. That's when trouble with other kids started. Homophobia, I suppose they'd call it these days. I was the kid they jokingly called a homo. Nothing too bad, never to my face, just comments I heard from time to time. I used to go to the school dances and I even dated girls but I was still called a homo. One day, this new kid arrived and he was mean spirited. I mean he did awful things. Pushed me around, said horrible things, made fun of me.

"My mother, when I told her, would sympathise and my father would tell me to thump him. 'One shot to the nose, Ian, and that'll be the end of it. I'll teach you how to box, boy.' He was always berating my mother for making me into a Mummy's boy, until one day, sick of him and sick of my tormentor, I took him up on his offer."

Father Ward laughed. "My father went all out. Punching bag, gloves, skipping rope, weights, you name it. And every night, he'd work with me. I was no boxer. Jabs, feints, hooks, upper-cuts, combinations. I knew the names far better than I could execute them. And every day, I'd see this kid at school and tried to imagine actually fighting him. It just seemed like something I'd never be able to do. I'd taken on a Sisyphean task.

"But the funny thing is, as the weeks rolled by and my arms grew bigger, my chest harder and my breathing easier, I believed that maybe I could. By then, I was punching that bag hard. I mean really hard. Especially when I used a left hook. My father would spar with me and tell me I wasn't to use the left hook on him. And one day, I said to this kid to back off, to leave me alone and he laughed. 'Or what?' I told him I'd fight him. You should have seen the look in his eyes. He immediately turned and told everyone. 'Ward wants to fight me.' It was a big joke. 'The poof wants to fight.'

"I told him I'd meet him around the back, after school, and that was his big joke for the rest of the day. He went around telling everyone. In fact, he thought it was such a joke I didn't expect him to turn up. But he did, and he was just as surprised to see me.

"After he'd finished smirking at how easy it was going to be, he went down into a wrestler's crouch and started circling me, taunting me, telling me he was ready anytime I had the guts to make a move. So I stepped into him and drove in a left hook. It knocked him over on his side. Knocked all the smugness out of him, too. 'Hey,' he said, 'that's not wrestling.' I just smiled at that and went after him. Had him going backwards. It was easy work.

"Word went around and from that day on no one at the school ever called me a poof or a homo, except for one person. And that person was me. Because I knew that's what

I really was. A homosexual." He spread out his hands and patted the air. "Not what Pope Francis would call 'a strong homosexual orientation.' But definitely that way inclined. As I say, I had girlfriends. I could have married and had children. But being honest with myself, homosexuality is my natural orientation. Which is not to say it's a problem to me as a priest. It isn't. I practice the same custody of the eyes, the same prayers for chastity, the same resistance to temptation that a good and chaste heterosexual priest would practice." He paused and, for the first time, looked at his listener. The benign look on the old priest's face was something he would never forget. "So," he said, in conclusion, "thought I'd better tell you that one. Might be something used against me."

Father Gilbert agreed and was warm in his appreciation of Father Ward's humble honesty, but it was waved aside.

"There's one other thing," said Father Ward, "I often wonder if it's inappropriate I continue as a priest. Pope Benedict would certainly say so. In an interview, recorded for all to read on Google, he is adamant that any homosexual orientation should prevent the church from accepting a man as a priest. He argues that a priest must be able to give himself totally to the church as a married man gives himself totally to his wife. In particular, he's referring to paternity or fatherhood. A priest is supposed to give up paternity of children to offer that paternity to his flock. He cites a lack of male physical aggressiveness or immaturity that leads to a lack of firmness and perseverance. Such a priest, as I, in his opinion, is unsuitable for being in authority and guiding people because, to quote him, we are 'by nature self-pitying, overly sensitive and neurotic.'" He stopped and waited for Father Gilbert's response.

The older priest was not given to glib, patronising comments. He simply said, "Are you?"

"Am I self-pitying, overly sensitive and neurotic?"

Father Gilbert nodded.

"Sometimes."

Father Gilbert smiled and raised his eyebrows. "Welcome to the human race. The same moral weakness is in all of us, from what I've seen. And keep in mind what the Pope Francis is saying. He simply asks homosexual priests to do exactly what you're doing: remain celibate and act responsibly."

Father Ward was pale and sat back with a grave look on his face and Father Gilbert could see he had paid a big price for what he had shared. He cocked his head and gave Father Ward a smile. Then he laughed. "Ian," he said, "after what I'm going to share you're going to wish you'd gone second."

Father Ward frowned.

"As I told you, everything Dean Collins says is true. But he doesn't know all of it." He sighed and laughed again. "Wal Footrot. I like that. Your father and mine would have been good mates. My father worked at the Freezing Works. The union delegate. A tough negotiator, he had the respect of everyone." He laughed. "He was almost the complete antithesis of my dear mother. She had been educated at Baradene, that private Catholic school for girls from affluent families. She was the daughter of a wealthy farmer. Trained in elocution, the piano, correct deportment and manners, she had been educated with languages and literature and had all the refinement of a lady.

"Whereas my father was a working man with a working man's appetites and no appreciation for the arts, music or higher learning. He was rough, liked his beer and expected my mother to be the little lady who kept house and provided good meals. He also felt his inferiority to her and could be abusive if he sensed any disapproval. He'd been a big, handsome rugby man when he swept her off her feet and took her back to Taranaki to live with him. But there wasn't much love lost between them after a few years."

Before he could continue, Father Gilbert was interrupted by a long, loud knock at the back door. Father Ward went to answer it. A group of Maori were there.

"Kia ora, Pa."

"Morning, Kenny, how can I help you?"

"Pa, they're bringing my uncle's body back to the marae for the tangi."

"Yes, I know I'm doing the funeral."

"They left early this morning and will be there soon. My grandmother is pretty upset. She wants a priest there for when they arrive."

"Well, I ah . . ." Father Ward, having already arranged to say the funeral Mass, considered it a little rich to have to go to the tangi as well. It was important he stand his ground on this one or he would set a precedent. But before he could decline the request, Father Gilbert was there at his side, offering to go.

They received him warmly at the marae and the grieving mother took great comfort from his presence. He stayed on until late in the night, forgoing the offer of a mattress to sleep on, by pleading old bones and returned to the presbytery in the early hours of the morning.

The late night left him feeling ragged but he still made it out to the kitchen to join Father Ward for breakfast and reported to him on the events of the tangi. Father Ward poured him a cup of tea and listened without much enthusiasm, and Father Gilbert rightly read he was annoyed.

"Ian, I understand why you didn't want to go. A priest has to set limits if he's to survive here all on his own. But they seemed very earnest."

Father Ward closed his eyes and sighed. "So, you think I should've gone."

"No, I'm not saying that. But I think I should've gone. Relieving for priests around the Diocese over the years has taught me how sensitive people can be when they're grieving."

Father Ward folded his arms.

"You did well to open the door. It was after six o'clock."

Father Ward's eyes narrowed. He wasn't sure about the sincerity of this comment, even suspected a hint of sarcasm.

"I mean that sincerely," said Father Gilbert. "As I say, I understand why a sole charge priest would want to set limits. But when someone knocks at a presbytery door it should almost always be opened. Which doesn't mean to say you have to do what is being asked of you. It's the difference between setting up a barrier and setting boundaries."

Father Ward frowned.

"A subtle difference," said Father Gilbert. "Boundaries can be negotiated."

Father Ward gave no reaction to this. He was

thinking.

"Be that as it may, Ian, let me share a few examples of how sensitive people can be. An old woman dies. All her life has been about service to her parish. A brilliant singer and organist, she uses her gift almost every Sunday. She's there at every weekday Mass to clear the altar for the priest and arrange new flowers from her garden. She brings meals to the priests. And so on and so on. But in the last few years of her life, during the tenure of one priest, the last priest there before she dies, she suffers from dementia and does odd things: turning up to the presbytery in her pyjamas at three in the morning for Mass, muttering the priest's responses with him, taking the priest to task for things he has said in his sermon.

"Now at her funeral, in front of her family, gathered from all over the country, and prominent people in the community that priest dedicates most of his comments to the woman's odd behaviours in her last years, much to the fury of her immediate family, one of whom vows never to return to church again.

"At another funeral, a heartbroken widow, surrounded by her family, is struggling to cope with the loss of her husband of sixty years when the priest, seeking to console her, says, 'Oh well, Nancy, mustn't get too despondent, you still have the rest of your family to look after you. Consider yourself lucky. Not everyone has that.'

"And these are all stories related to me by people from this parish."

Father Ward frowned.

"And it's not just grieving people. Mothers can be touchy as well. While in town the other day, I recognised a woman who was a regular at Mass last time I was here. I happened to say, I hadn't seen her at Mass this time. Her eyes teared up and she couldn't speak. I thought she was going to walk off, but she managed to compose herself.

"This mother has six children. Prior to her signing up her youngest for the sacramental programme for his first Holy Communion, she had faithfully accompanied each of the other five, so she knew the programme well enough to give it at home. But, no, in obedience to the priest, not you by the way, Ian, she brought her youngest to each of the sessions except two, and, knowing this dear girl, there would have would been good reasons for missing those two. Anyway, when it came to practicing for the big event the priest took her aside and told her the child would not be able to receive Holy Communion with the others because he had missed two sessions."

"Oh, my goodness," said Father Ward, appalled.

"Exactly, Ian, and thank you for that response. I thought it was just me as an old missionary. You get someone interested in receiving the sacraments in the missions, you don't muck around, you initiate them there and then and the rest of it can come as you go along. I learned that pretty quick. They generally had a good idea if they came forward."

"I take your point," said Father Ward, "I'll work on discernment."

"You do alright, Father," said Father Gilbert, "no one complains about you. I've seen how carefully you relate to your parishioners but the point still stands, we all need reminding. And with all due respect to Pope Benedict, he would be well advised to direct some of his comments to the damage done by insensitive priests." He yawned. "Oh dear, I'm a wreck. Too old to be going out all hours. So much for my discernment." He shuffled over to the bread drawer took two pieces and loaded the toaster. He sat at the table to wait for them to cook. When the toaster popped, he was sound asleep, arms folded, sitting upright, his head lolling forward.

Father Ward buttered the toast, put it on a plate and took it over to him. When he set the plate in front of him, he awoke, with a start. "Oh dear, I think I went to sleep."

"You did," said Father Ward.

Father Gilbert took up a piece of toast and yawned. "Oh dear, I'm a wreck," he repeated.

"Tangis will do that to you," said Father Ward and smiled.

Any thought Father Ward had of hearing more of Father Gilbert's personal story was put to rest as the house reverberated with his snoring for the rest of that afternoon. He did manage to rouse himself for an evening meal but then went straight to bed.

Chapter Thirteen

Father Gilbert arose refreshed the next morning. After Mass and his walk down to the town, he was ready to sit down to one of Father Ward's cappuccinos and continue his story.

"I was the oldest of five and, as the oldest are, I felt a responsibility to compensate for Dad's treatment of our mother. I soon saw that doing well at school was what pleased her best. It wasn't hard, with a mother like her to help. Before starting high school, I knew the five Latin declensions, the four conjugations and had a considerable vocabulary. I always came first in Latin. And perhaps that was the beginning of my vocation, but I think it was earlier than that.

"We used to have Columbans visit the Catholic primary school I attended. They would set up a film projector in the school hall and show films. And I was spellbound. These guys were real men, going off into harsh lands risking imprisonment and martyrdom and they were calling for other men to join the battle and take on the adventure and it stirred something deep in me.

"I was one of the first students to attend Francis Douglas College, a Catholic high school named after a Columban priest, killed by the Japanese for refusing to break the seal of confession. The Japanese beat him to death and he never uttered a word. That kind of heroism resonated with me. When I told my dad I wanted to join the Columbans he never said a bad word. They had his respect too, and that was big.

"So off I went to Sydney. Seventeen years old. Straight out of school. In those days, Columban missionaries were trained in Sydney. Americans, Irishmen, New Zealanders and Australians. We all trained there. Liberation theology was the in-thing. It was new and exciting and I loved the idea of a preferential option for the poor. They sent me off to South America and then they reassigned me to help set up a new missionary centre in the rural part of Lahore, Pakistan. I enjoyed South America. The faith was strong and we were appreciated. Pakistan was different.

"Bhutto, the former president, had been executed

after a military takeover and the new government was promoting Islam. And there I was being sent to promote Christianity. I remember being interviewed back in my hometown before leaving. I told the reporter we no longer had the old colonial approach to mission work. Instead, we were looking for mutual enrichment, to learn from the people and share their experience while helping them to live a more human and therefore Christian life."

He shook his head. "I told the reporter that we had lost our arrogance. But we hadn't. The idea we could make a difference was still arrogant. We weren't going to set up medical or teaching services. We were going to live alongside them. 'We'll be doing a lot of waiting, watching and listening', I told the reporter. *Missionary Work Enters New Era*, they titled it and my mother kept that article among her personal affects until the day she died. I burned it when I found it.

"Pakistan taught me who I was. 'A humble knowledge of thyself is a surer way to God than a deep search after learning', writes Thomas a Kempis. That country humbled me in a way that eventually did my priesthood more good than all those years of study at the seminary. I say eventually because it took a long time. Anyway, mustn't get ahead of myself. I arrived at the height of summer. The heat was enough to boil a man's blood. Forty-six degrees. By the time I walked from the airport terminal to a taxi, I was saturated.

"The quality of the air was so bad my eyes were smarting the moment I stepped out of the taxi. And the noise . . . The drivers of the trucks and the buses and the rickshaws who live with it every day suffer permanent hearing problems.

"There were people everywhere. More people than I've ever seen in one place in my life. More than the population of New Zealand crammed into the place, thirty percent of them in slums. And the stink of raw sewerage running through those slums . . ." He closed his eyes at the memory of it.

"I was all buoyed with the heroism of the missionary call, but the reality of what I had stepped into was . . . I hated being there. It was barely tolerable. And we had set ourselves up to live among the poorest of the poor. The lowest caste. The untouchables. The landless peasants. The sanitation workers. These were the descendants of those who had accepted the apostle Thomas' call to Christianity. For obvious reasons. They were despised and looked down upon and Saint Thomas was telling them Jesus loved them, that in His eyes they were important.

"And every day, five times a day, the imams blasted out the call to prayer from speakers all over the city. Sometimes, as early as three in the morning. Like a constant reminder that Islam owned the place and no other religion was going to get a look in. Catholics made up less than three quarters of a percent. The Government may not have outlawed Christianity but the writings of the prophet, in the Koran, had. 'There is only one way to God. Infidels must accept conversion or die.' I arrived in the years before Islamic militants attacked and destroyed Christian churches but you could see it coming.

"I had been tasked with playing Sibelius's violin concerto without ever having learned the violin. So what did a young Kiwi priest so far from home do to cope? He had a few beers, mate. The presbytery boasted a good supply of alcohol. Every time we had a visitor, they brought in duty free alcohol for us. So I went to work realising my innate potential for full blown alcoholism, following in the footsteps of my dear old dad. That helped, together with a calendar in my room on which I marked off the days, weeks and months before I could fly back home. Six years I lasted in that hell hole. And every year my trolley at duty free carried more and more.

"Then one year, I just couldn't go back. The missionary idealism in me was dead. I had wrestled with the idea for most of my last year there and when I arrived home I knew I wasn't going back. Don't get me wrong, the people we served were grateful for the sacraments. We had something to give. I knew it wasn't entirely wasted effort." Father Gilbert sighed. "When I told my superiors I wasn't going back, they offered me a teaching position at the seminary. It's what they did back then. Appointed you for life to a mission and if you couldn't take it they offered you a teaching position."

He laughed. "I was the priest who was drunk by five in the afternoon and they were offering me a job teaching seminarians. I wasn't ready to accept I had a drinking problem. That was just something I did in Pakistan and who could blame me. That's how my thinking went.

"But apart from that, my real problem was my failure to ever completely commit to the priesthood. I was always open to the idea of a relationship with a woman. Always saw it as a possibility if the right woman came along. Never closed the door on that. And looking back, I recognise that failure to commit one hundred percent made me vulnerable whenever doubts came in. I always had the thought that maybe I could be happier in a relationship. I knew nothing of women, of course. There were girls at the convent school I went to. But Francis Douglas was all boys. I went into the seminary straight from school. No experience of the world whatsoever."

He smiled. "Looking at me now you may find it hard to believe but women seemed attracted to me. We had a very open seminary there in Sydney and women would come in to visit. You know relations of seminarians and friends of relations; and it was clear some of them were out to get a man and they let you know they liked you. Whether I like to admit it or not I had stored that as a fall-back option and it made leaving easier. When I told my superiors, I wanted to leave no one tried to talk me out of it.

"I don't know how I thought I was going to support myself. The training we receive as priests doesn't hold much value in the workplace. I was in my thirties with no real qualifications and no money in the bank. But I found odd jobs here and there, mainly as a labourer and eventually settled for painting. It was boring and tedious and not all that well paid. I could only afford to stay in some pretty grotty places. And there were some nights there, between places, when as I've said I slept with the drunks under Grafton Bridge.

"Eventually I got into a relationship with a woman I met in the pub and we took a flat together. And she became pregnant. My son was born and her parents took him off us, which was a good thing. We were hopeless. A couple of drunks. We split up not long after. I would go and visit my boy, David, until one day his grandparents told me I wasn't welcome if I had been drinking. It was the wake-up call I needed. I wanted to be a good father. That was the moment when the penny dropped. Like one of James Joyce's epiphanies. I was too much of a drunk to be a decent father. Just like my father. Just like the man I swore I'd never be."

"Goodness me," said Father Ward, "I should've let you go first."

"Yep."

They both chuckled.

Father Ward drew breath and went to speak, then he exhaled in a long, slow breath, wondering where to start. "So . . . Now you're a holy priest. The diocesan exorcist."

"I wouldn't go that far. I have no idea how many priests the bishop asked before he gave me the job. Not a job many want for some reason."

"But you said yes."

Father Gilbert nodded. "I owed the bishop. He'd given me a second chance. An alcoholic with a child out of wedlock. It was a big ask."

"What made you go back to the priesthood?"

"Good question. The simple answer: God still wanted me. I had this vague uneasiness about what I was doing. I wasn't doing anything bad. The painting business was going well. I was seeing David on a regular basis and saving for my own place. But there was little joy in it, no peace and contentment. I know now God was calling me back, but at the time I never gave that a thought. I mean how could God ever entrust me with being a priest again. A drunk who had lived with down-and-outs. I was the whiskey priest with a child, for goodness sake. The deep sense of shame and unworthiness was just too much. I couldn't forgive myself and I didn't expect God to either. I was back attending Mass and going to confession, but the idea of ever being a priest again, that was a bridge too far.

"Then one Sunday, the Gospel was that story of the Lord's first encounter with Peter and the apostles. You'll remember they'd been fishing and caught nothing and the Lord told them to try again and they pulled in so many fish their boats almost sunk and Peter says to Jesus, 'Depart from me, for I am a sinful man.' And I knew exactly what Peter felt because that was exactly what I was saying to the Lord about the call back to priesthood. But the Lord still wanted Peter and I knew at that moment he was saying the same thing to me. The sense of His love for me, His mercy, His kindness was so overwhelming tears streamed down my face. Fortunately, I was right at the back of the church. No one saw me and I left.

"I was in the habit of going to confession to an old Dominican and I shared what happened. He recommended I go on retreat, a personal retreat he would oversee. And every day, when we met, this old priest would talk about God's love and mercy. He reminded me of other men whom God had called. Men like Augustine, a womanizer, father to an illegitimate son who abandoned a lover of fifteen years to marry an heiress. And Peter the apostle who denied Him three times and was chosen as the head of His church. And King David who bedded Bathsheba, another man's wife, and arranged for that man to be sent to the front of the fighting to be killed. Murder and adultery and God forgave David, allowed him back. And Saint Paul, the former Pharisee, who had been present at the brutal stoning of Stephen and entirely approved. It was a strong argument. During that retreat I felt

God calling me back even more strongly. At the end of it, my old Dominican confessor arranged a meeting with the bishop.

"The bishop was canny. There were hoops to jump through. He sent me to Broom in Western Australia to live with a tough old priest as part of the discernment process. I think that was supposed to put me off, but it didn't. I came back, still keen and they allowed me to stay in the presbytery in Remuera. I went out to work as a painter during the day and came home to be with the priests at night. Eventually, the bishop gave me the nod.

"When I first set out as a young priest, it was all about me and what I had to offer. When I set out that second time, it was all about God and what he had to offer. God had restored me back to sanity from an unmanageable life, broken by sin and my whole life was dependent on Him. I had been humbled. When I came back, I stood before His people as a fellow sinner wanting to be holy as He is holy, wanting to make amends for what I have done. So, there you have it, Graham Greene's whiskey priest in the flesh. Not too shocking, I hope."

"Not at all. I did wonder why you didn't drink."

"Well wonder no more, Ian. And just to be clear, you're a good priest. Don't let anyone tell you differently. I've known a few bad priests, myself included. Patriarchal, insensitive, stupid, arrogant men who drive people from our churches. As the good Pope says we are running a field hospital for the wounded. It's not a country club for the perfect. And wounded people relate better to humility than pride."

Chapter Fourteen

Days passed and still no word came from the Alexanders. The time of waiting no longer weighed so heavily on Father Ward. He was enjoying Father Gilbert's company and whenever he came back from making visitations in the parish, he was keen to share. On one particular afternoon, he returned excited. "I've been visiting some of the wealthier members of the parish," he told Father Gilbert.

"Oh, yes," said Father Gilbert, imagining Father Ward being more at home with the rich but reserving his judgment.

"Yes, I've been asking for money."

Father Gilbert chuckled.

"Not for us of course, for the Ramekas and families like them."

"The Ramekas?"

"The big man who came in my absence. The idea is to establish a scholarship for children of good character who would like to attend our school. The response has been good."

Telling their personal stories and sharing the events of the day had created an understanding and appreciation of each other and the younger priest was more forthcoming in sharing his reservations and concerns about the priesthood. The difficulty he had preaching sermons was one of those concerns.

"I've always been loath to cause offence and have relied on people coming to an understanding of their error in certain matters by being less than direct in my approach and that has carried through to my sermons," said Father Ward. The two priests were seated in the lounge. They had shared with one another the events of the day and, as had become their want, they were sharing philosophies on aspects of priesthood.

"I know what you mean," said Father Gilbert. "There is an argument for it. Tell all the truth but tell it slant – Success in Circuit lies,"

"Too bright for our infirm Delight," continued Father Ward, nodding.

"How does the rest go? Been a while since I read Emily."

"The Truth's superb surprise. As Lightning to the Children eased."

"Ah, yes, yes," said Father Gilbert, his memory jogged, "With explanation kind

The Truth must dazzle gradually."

"Or every man be blind," concluded Father Ward.

"Mmm," said Father Gilbert, "you have a generous appreciation of your congregation, Ian, but from what I see subtlety may be lost on them."

"I've wondered that myself."

"The problem with priests is our intellects. We forget the man in the street, the man in the pews on Sunday, he likes it plain and simple. When I first arrived in Lahore, my first job was learning Urdu. Then I set myself the job of giving my congregation the benefit of all my philosophy and theology in Urdu. A real *tour de force* I can tell you. But I soon realised they didn't have a clue what I was talking about. I left the pulpit every Sunday thinking I was the new Saint Thomas Aquinas and they left church every Sunday completely confused. Plain and simple, Ian. Tell them what you're going to tell them. Tell them again. And then tell them what you just told them. Repetition, that's the key. They might just remember that way."

"And avoiding giving offence?"

"Well, there's giving offence and there's giving offence," said Father Gilbert. "But as for the truth? If that gives offence, we need to remember it's the Truth and God is Truth, so He'll sort it. The Truth is a health-giving medicine, however difficult it may be for some of them to swallow."

"You make it sound easy."

"It isn't. We're in Enemy territory, Ian. Warriors called by God to fight on his behalf."

"Warriors," repeated Father Ward. "Not sure I'd characterise myself in that way."

"All warriors have to work on being a warrior, Father Ward. The natural inclination of every man, every priest, is to take the line of least resistance, to avoid trouble, avoid giving offence. Anything that invades his comfort zone. We all have that to contend with. We're all Adam's sons, all born with original sin."

"Well," said Father Ward, pouring another glass of port, "it seems to come easy to you."

Father Gilbert scoffed at that. "I don't have much to thank my old dad for but I do thank him for what he taught me about being brave. They didn't call him Bull Gilbert for nothing. He never backed down from trouble. In fact, he would go to meet it, head on. And that's what he taught me. On one of the rare occasions he came to watch me play rugby, he noticed I avoided tackling big players and he took me aside and he said, 'A brave tackle is a hard tackle, Peter, but the more you do it the braver you become. The trick is to move in hard and quick before they build up a head of steam. Always go to meet trouble, Peter. Don't hang back from it. Man up and the man in you will grow.'"

"Man up and the man in you will grow," repeated Father Ward, "that's got a ring to it alright."

"And it works. Doesn't have to be something big. You pay someone to mow your lawns. He doesn't do it properly. You tell him. A tyre man quotes you one hundred to fit and supply a tyre then wants to charge you a hundred and twenty. You insist on the original quote. Someone carries on with racist comments. You tell him racism is offensive. Someone lies to you and you know it. You tell him."

"Not how to win friends and influence people," said Father Ward.

"Not everyone will like you. But they'll respect you. This is who I am, I'm not giving you a false version of me is what you're saying. It's that Truth again. Healing but not always palatable."

Father Ward did what he always did when considering something: he averted his eyes and took a long moment and then came back to his old friend, nodding his head and Father Gilbert continued, "Too many men these days take your approach, the nice and inoffensive approach. They never take on trouble, just roll with it and the man in them shrinks until they're just the quiet presence in the pews no one seems to notice. Look around next Sunday."

Father Ward was too preoccupied with his sermon to look around the following Sunday. The Gospel for the day was about Christ separating the sheep from the goats at the last judgment. He mounted the steps to his pulpit and took a long breath, glancing at Father Gilbert who had just sat after reading the Gospel. The older priest was smiling encouragingly. A child was making a noisy fuss. Father Ward turned to the congregation, "Okay, little one, I promise I shall be brief."

The parishioners laughed. Father Ward could almost count on one hand the number of times he had made them laugh and he took that as a good sign.

"I have to be brief. I'm under orders to be brief," he continued. "Our dear Holy Father in a recent address to priests has given us a directive, 'Make your sermons brief.' Because he doesn't want you leaving church with a long face. He wants you leaving with joy."

Another ripple of polite laughter.

"Today we are reminded of the last judgment. And for those of you who may have an idea of God who is so benign He will admit all to heaven, take pause. There is a heaven and there is a hell and there is a purgatory." He himself paused a long moment. He was breaking new ground here and he could feel himself shaking. This was not the usual inoffensive love sermon.

"Sobering I know. But there is also comfort in knowing justice will eventually be served. As a priest, I often have to deal with the pain and suffering caused by men who seem to get away with what they have done. Remember the 2008 Global Financial Crisis. So many of those who had trusted financiers with their life savings suffered. And yet those responsible seemed to get away with it. The five directors of Equitycorp were found guilty and received sentences of one to three and a half years in minimum security prisons, where I'm told, they were allowed out on weekend leave." He paused a long moment.

"The fortunes they had accumulated were safely squirrelled away in trusts and couldn't be touched. And, to add insult to injury, they applied for and were granted legal aid. Their legal fees were paid for by the taxpayer. A million dollars I am told. They had destroyed people's lives, people who had trusted them and yet they seemed to get off so lightly."

He stopped again to take in all the stern faces. "Doesn't it make you angry?" Heads nodded. "My dear people, take comfort, there is another tribunal awaiting those men.

"To all of you who have suffered injustice and seen the perpetrator seem to get away with it, remember: there is another tribunal.

"To the man or woman whose spouse has been unfaithful and has endured the anguish of dealing with lawyers and courts and suffered the loss of home or business or children and feels let down by our justice system . . . there is another tribunal.

"To the parents of the child killed by a drunken driver running a red light, denied justice, after sitting through court and listening to clever lawyers pleading mitigating circumstances, there is another tribunal.

"To those of you who have had their homes burgled, your private space violated, and precious things taken and not recovered and seen those responsible walk free from court, there is another tribunal.

"I could go on and on, until eventually I have named

enough injustices to include each and every one of you as a victim because, as sure as I am standing here, I know each and every one of you has suffered some form of injustice in your lifetime. You're not alone and there is another tribunal.

"To those of you, impatient for that tribunal, tempted to take matters into your own hands, remember the words of Our Blessed Lord, 'Vengeance is mine.' And here I speak to those among us who, like me, stand opposed to abortion and would like to close the clinics down by force."

A young woman sitting at the back of the church suddenly raised her head and stared him down with a look of thunder and Father Ward felt it like a physical blow and faltered.

He steeled himself and brought his sermon to a conclusion. "For here again we must put our trust in God to see justice done. And He will. My dear people, there is another tribunal." He nodded in conclusion and sat down beside Father Gilbert while the ushers took in the collection.

Father Ward was very adept at picking up any abreaction to his sermons. It was the reason his sermons, until that morning, rarely gave offence. He had learned to tailor them with that criterion in mind. In short, he had learned that so long as he preached on love in a bland, generic way, no offence was given.

If he had not made the reference to abortions, he would have received nothing but plaudits that morning. There was a warm acceptance of what he had said and many like the two women whose husbands were seeking divorces went out of their way to thank him after Mass.

When he saw the young woman hanging around in the foyer, watching him, he fully expected her to try and have words with him. But here he was saved by his demanding Sunday Mass schedule and was hurrying to another Mass centre before she could corner him. He had not recognised the young woman as a regular Mass-goer and mistakenly believed it unlikely their paths would cross again.

Chapter Fifteen

Harry Alexander knocked at the presbytery door late that Sunday afternoon. Father Ward had delivered his sermon at all the Mass centres and Father Gilbert had been warm in his approval. It had been, by and large, a good day for the young priest and, in a spirit of celebration, he was in the kitchen preparing his specialty, lasagna. He paused in his preparation, in the hope Father Gilbert might answer the door. Harry knocked again and Father Ward, accepting the inevitable, went to see who it was.

"Is the old priest here?" asked Harry, clearly agitated and in a hurry.

Father Gilbert, who had dozed off in the lounge, took a minute to come to his senses and slowly climb out of his chair. He was still somewhat befuddled by sleep when he encountered Harry at the door but saw immediately Harry was worked up.

"Father, we need you to come as soon as possible," said the farmer quickly, "Mark is not good and something needs to be done."

"Alright, Harry, you'd better come in," said Father Gilbert and opened the door for the farmer. The other man seemed reluctant to tarry but deferred to the older priest and took off his gumboots and followed meekly into the priests' kitchen. "Would you like a cup of tea?" asked Father Ward.

"No, I need to get back. Doesn't pay to leave him on his own."

"And your wife?"

"She's not there. I've taken her to her sister's down the road. She wasn't coping. I was worried about her."

"And she doesn't mind us helping Mark?"

"She's in no state to say, Father." He took a big breath. "She got to the end of her tether. Yesterday, she couldn't get out of bed. Almost too weak to sit up. I had to help her to the bathroom. Her sister's a nurse. She says Sandra's exhausted."

"What's been happening, Harry?" asked Father Ward.

Harry took a moment and stared down at the hat he was holding in his hands. "More of what I told Father Gilbert here, but worse. Mark's not eating now and he's getting weaker. I think he wants help. I just get that idea. Today my brother and I tried to feed him something. It was awful. He was curled up into a ball and then he uncurled as my brother came in the room and his tongue started flicking in and out. My brother, Kevin, he's older than me. Never been afraid of anything. He's the one you call when a bull is causing trouble. But he was ginger about approaching Mark after what he saw, I tell you. All this writhing and screaming and hissing and cursing really gave Kevin the willies. Kevin's a strong man, Father. He usually wins top axeman at the A and P show each year, but he was struggling to hold Mark."

"What gives you the idea Mark wants help, Harry?"

"Every now and then it's like he's there. Hard to explain. Like I said before it's in the eyes. And the way he looks at me. I think he's had enough."

Father Gilbert explained what they would do. He advised Harry to take the sacrament of reconciliation and he agreed. Then he gave him instructions and undertook to be at his place the following morning, after Mass.

Father Ward was concerned about the timing. He could see his fellow priest had been wearied by the demands of parish life and counselled a few days' rest.

"These things are never convenient, Ian. When I am weak, I am strong. The less I have to give the more the Lord will have to step into the breach." He laughed at the young priest's look of concern. "We'll be fine, Ian. But let's spend as much of this night in prayer as we can. We also need to confess our sins to one another and concelebrate Mass tomorrow. The idea is to bring Christ's presence with us and clear ourselves of anything that might hinder that."

The young woman from the Sunday Mass returned the next day. She arrived toward the end of Mass and stayed in the foyer of the church, legs crossed, arms folded, face tight with resolve. The daily Mass-goers came out and offered her a cup of tea, but she was in no mood for their hospitality and brushed them aside. She wanted to see the priest and went and stood outside the sacristy to wait.

Father Ward was the first to emerge and she went straight up to him. She was loud and aggressive and wasn't concerned who was listening. "I'm here to talk to you about your sermon yesterday."

"Would you like to come into the church and take a seat there?"

"No, here's fine. I want to know more of your views are on abortion."

"I have the view of the church," said Father Ward, frowning and somewhat taken aback.

"Which is?"

"We support life and the child's right to live."

The young woman snorted her contempt. "And a woman's right to choose what happens to her body is a sin, right?"

Father Ward did not respond.

"Oh, I know what you priests would have us believe is a sin. I was raised a Catholic. I've been through your brain washing. And I'm here to tell you that if it's a sin it's a gender biased sin. You people make women bear all the blame and hardship for unwanted pregnancies and say nothing about the responsibility of men."

In defence of their priest, the ladies enjoying a cup of tea had raised the volume of their conversation.

"This is really not the time or place. I . . ." said Father Ward before he was loudly interrupted.

"Using a woman's body as a receptacle for an unwanted pregnancy is just as unethical as a termination."

"Excuse me, young lady, but I really think that . . ." One of the old ladies had stepped in to intervene, when the young woman turned on her as well.

"No, I won't excuse you. I don't need to be hearing from a priest's toady. It's women like you," and here she gestured to all the women at the kitchen serviery, "that perpetuate the exclusively male clergy connected to abuse in the church."

"I beg your pardon," said the old woman, "how dare

you?"

"Ladies," said Father Ward putting his hand up, but the young woman was not to be silenced and bore down on the old woman. "This Catholic Church is a patriarchal church and women like you allow priests power over you and over young, vulnerable, subordinate males. None of you have the courage to stand up to them and your silence condones their culture of authoritarianism and misogyny."

Father Gilbert had stepped out of the sacristy and was quietly closing the door while the young woman was speaking. He turned to her and said, "Hello, Matilda." The young woman, somewhat nonplussed by this old priest calling her by name, frowned. "I've been listening and you certainly have my attention." He turned to the old ladies. "We won't be needing a cup of tea this morning, ladies," he said. He nodded to Father Ward who took that as his cue to leave as well.

Intrigued by the old priest who knew her name, Matilda folded her arms and sealed her lips tight, taking in the measure of the old man. When they were alone, Father Gilbert smiled and looked her warmly in the eye. "You have great courage coming here like this."

"Don't patronise me!"

"Heaven forbid. I meant that most sincerely."

"Who are you?" she asked.

"Father Gilbert."

"How do you know my name?" she asked.

"One of the ladies. I heard her mention it."

"And I don't need to ask what your views on abortion are," she said contemptuously.

Father Gilbert took a big breath, closed his eyes and

rubbed his gammy leg. “Look, do you mind if we take a seat over by the window in the sun. My old bones.”

“Why?”

“I want to hear what you have to say,” he said leading her slowly across the foyer where she refused to sit and stood eyeing him fiercely.

“I want to know why you are so angry,” said Father Gilbert and Matilda laughed loudly and contemptuously.

Father Gilbert waited and seeing he was sincere in wanting to know her views, she sat down and launched forth, though less stridently.

Half an hour later, Matilda emerged from the foyer and drove off. Father Gilbert sat at the window a while longer enjoying the warm sun only to be interrupted by Father Ward, concerned at the urgency of the morning’s work.

They travelled out to the Alexanders in Father Gilbert’s old Ford. The exchange with Matilda occupied their thoughts for a while and they travelled in silence. “Apparently that young woman was never any trouble before she went to university,” said Father Ward.

“Often the way,” said Father Gilbert.

“If she was open to listening, I would point out we call our church Mother Church and remind her of our devotion to Mary. If she was open,” said Father Ward.

“Yes.”

“Have to admire her courage, though. That little exchange would’ve cost her a lot.”

“Oh, I’m sure it did,” Father Gilbert agreed.

Father Ward sighed. “I’m not very good at dealing with confrontational people. They’re rare but they get me on the back foot every time."

"You did fine, Ian."

"You spent a while talking to her."

"Listening," Father Gilbert corrected. "Men have a lot to answer for. My own father was a very domineering, abusive man. It's not hard for me to understand a woman like Matilda."

"Yes," said Father Ward.

"Now," said Father Gilbert, changing the subject, "I think you'll like this." He switched his tape deck on and Debussy's Reverie played.

It was a beautiful day. Rain had recently fallen and the pasture on either side of the road was green and lush. The warm air of a summer's clear morning came through the open windows. Father Gilbert had spent most of the night in prayer and was pale with fatigue. He had also fasted from breakfast. But he was smiling in appreciation of the music and the beautiful day. "Beauty is truth and truth is beauty. That is all you know and all you need to know," he said.

"John Keats," said Father Ward, frowning.

Father Gilbert nodded, aware Father Ward was feeling the burden of what they were setting out to do. "Anything bizarre we see at the Alexanders is not truth, Ian. It's a lie. A distortion. A fabrication of what is real to distract us from the truth. It will unsettle you but stand firm. Remember the beauty of this day, the beauty of this music. That is truth. That is God. And that is what we are trying to restore."

Father Ward nodded earnestly and frowned.

"You alright?" asked Father Gilbert.

Father Ward's smile did not carry to his eyes. They

showed fear and dread.

"Don't worry, I'm nervous, too," said Father Gilbert. "Only to be expected from a couple of mere mortals like us."

Father Gilbert's admission of fear did not help and as they grew nearer the Alexanders, Father Ward repeated to himself his old school's motto: *confortare esto vir* (take courage and be a man), as he often did in anticipation of situations requiring courage. He was aware this was his second chance and he was full of resolve to stand his ground.

The farmhouse was down a long drive and Father Gilbert had to negotiate large potholes from the recent heavy rain. A dead macrocarpa hedge along the drive looked bleak against the blue sky of summer. The house was an unpretentious, sturdy weatherboard construction, made from kauri, milled on the farm by the original owner. It sat in the shadow of some pine trees, where a magpie was squawking at their intrusion. Surrounding the house was a wire mesh fence set against concrete posts.

Parking the car, the priests walked through a gate in the fence that groaned on its hinges and made their way up a cracked concrete path past an empty kennel. There were old cow bones and muddy holes near the unoccupied kennel. All the curtains in the house were drawn and no one came to answer their knock. A voice called out, "He's over at the shed. I've let him know you're here." The voice had come from the back of an old implement shed, near the house and a powerfully built man, in a black singlet emerged, wiping oil and grease from his hands, one of which he extended to Father Gilbert. "Kevin Alexander," he said and shook hands with both the priests.

He led them around the side of the house and was

pointing out Mark's shed at the bottom of the property when Harry Alexander arrived. There was no offer of hospitality. "We've set him up in the shed down here," said Harry leading them down a path. His brother, pulling back his shoulders, drew breath and followed. They stopped outside the door while the priests put on their surplices and purple stoles.

Father Gilbert handed the two men a pair of rosary beads and a copy of the Catholic rite of exorcism. "The responses are all clearly marked. If these demons try to distract us and slow things down, say the rosary. If I pause to exercise Christ's authority, say the rosary." He held up the cross. "All power is in the name of Jesus Christ, but the rosary is a form of torture. Consider the rosary beads like lashing this presence with barbed wire. And whatever happens, whatever you see, stay with the job."

The two farmers looked at each other.

"Jesus Christ has the authority," Father Gilbert assured them. "He will have the victory. Ignore the manifestations. Concentrate on God's power at work and the prayer of the church."

The air inside the unventilated shed was stale and the priests baulked at the lingering smell of excrement. They peered into what seemed an impenetrable darkness as Harry made his way across the concrete floor to draw back the curtains. There was an eerie silence and as light filtered into the room, they could see Mark staring at them all intently. When Father Gilbert approached him, he drew in on himself, growling and snarling. The old priest traced the sign of the cross over him and then the others. He nodded to Father Ward who sprinkled them all with holy water from an aspergillum. Mark's eyes went to the back of his head and he clawed at himself.

Father Gilbert knelt at the foot of the bed and recited the first name in a litany of the saints and gave the lead in making the appropriate response: "Lord have mercy."

The others did not take his lead. Father Ward was too taken aback by the demonic transformation in Mark's physical appearance. Pale and thin, he barely resembled the young man he had visited only weeks earlier. His skin like parchment was grey. His black hair stood on end, framing a face that seemed longer and thinner - a face with steepled brows, ferocious, bloodshot eyes and yellowed, sharp teeth, with prominent canines. The two farmers were distracted by the chilling cold inside the shed. Harry Alexander was zipping up his jacket and his brother Kevin was putting on a jersey he had wrapped around his waist in anticipation.

"Lord, have mercy," repeated Father Gilbert impatiently and the other three, now reading from their copy of the rite, hurried in on their response: "Lord, have mercy."

As the litany proceeded, Mark was shaking, his breathing quick and shallow.

"From all evil, deliver us, O Lord," said Father Gilbert.

"Deliver us, O Lord," responded the others.

"From all sin."

"Deliver us, O Lord."

Mark stared malevolently but made no sound until Father Gilbert said, "From all lewdness," and there was cynical laughter. So unnerving was it, the other three did not read their response.

"From all lewdness," repeated Father Gilbert.

"Deliver us, O Lord," the others intoned in quick unison.

At the end of the long list of invocations, Father Gilbert started in on more prayers, "Do not keep in mind, O Lord, our offences or those of our parents, nor take vengeance."

He was interrupted by a deep growling voice speaking in Latin. "*A puero patrem. Non es sacerdos.*" (The father of a child is not a priest) "*Nihil habes virtuem, senis.*" (You have no power, old man.)

Father Gilbert raised the cross and replied in Latin: "*Adjure te spiritus nequissime, per Deum omnipotentum.*" (I abjure you, most evil spirit by Almighty God.)

Mark rose up off the bed, hissing and growling, his tongue flicking in and out.

The temperature in the room was dropping and Mark slumped back on the bed, his head tilted at an unnatural angle, his eyes rolling to the back of his head. Father Ward was overtaken by spasms of shaking and he wrapped his arms around himself in an effort to control them. Mark's eyes flicked open and bore in on him. It was a moment of truth for the young priest, but he did not falter. He raised the cross higher and when Mark laughed he moved in closer and raised the volume of his responses.

Father Gilbert was now commanding the unclean spirit who had spoken to reveal his name, "I bind you and I command you, unclean spirit, whoever you are, along with your minions now attacking this servant of God, tell me your name."

"*Malo mori quam foedari,*" (Death before dishonour) chanted the unclean spirit and Father Gilbert faltered, taken by surprise by what the demon had said. The unclean spirit recognised this and came up off the bed. Collecting himself, Father Gilbert now attempted to lay his hands on Mark's head but was pushed aside and sent sprawling. Mark stood menacingly over the top of the old priest and Harry and Kevin quickly moved forward to offer protection but there was no need.

Mark withdrew and then, taking off his pyjama pants, he crouched down, in a squatting position and emptied his bowels. A suffocating stench pervaded the room. Harry went outside and brought in a bucket of water and a rag. He and his brother took Mark in hand to clean him up in what appeared a well-practiced procedure. There was no resistance from Mark until they attempted to put his pyjama pants back on. Neither of the two farmers could control him but the show of enormous strength was short lived and he sat on the bed while they finished the job.

Father Gilbert stood above him. "Tell me your name," he said loudly, "I command you, moreover, to obey me to the letter, I who am a minister of God despite my unworthiness; nor shall you be emboldened to harm in any way this creature of God, or the bystanders, or any of their possessions."

There was no response.

"Tell me your name!"

Father Ward moved in beside Father Gilbert and whispered in his ear. He was worried. Mark's breathing was barely audible. "He seems very weak," he said.

Father Gilbert laid his hand on Mark's forehead and prayed: "They shall lay their hands upon the sick and all will be well with them. May Jesus, Son of Mary, Lord and

Saviour of the world, through the merits and intercession of His holy apostles Peter and Paul and all His saints, show your favour and mercy."

Emboldened by Father Gilbert being able to lay his hand upon Mark without any reaction, Father Ward now reached down to check the pulse in Mark's arm. Immediately, Mark sat up growling and launched himself at the priest, fastening on to his arm with his teeth.

Father Ward cried out in horror and pulled back.

"*Tangunt me impune lacessit turpem homosexual*." (Touch me not with impunity, homosexual), snarled the demon and Mark dropped back on the bed, breathing heavily.

Father Ward's hand was dripping blood.

"That wound needs to be dressed, Father," said Harry, leading the priest away from the bed. "I've been bitten, too. Comes up real nasty if not seen to straight away."

Mark's eyes flicked open. He was smiling. "The boy is exhausted, priest. You are killing him." It was another voice, sinister and smarmy. "You must stop. We will leave."

Harry grabbed Father Gilbert's arm, shaking his head in response at what the demon was telling the priest.

Mark turned now to face Father Ward. He was taking off his pyjama pants again and making a lewd suggestion. It was yet another voice, slimy and sycophantic.

Father Ward had rolled back the sleeve of his surplice and Harry was staunching the flow of blood from the bite on his arm, with a handkerchief.

The new demonic voice continued to make lewd suggestions and Father Gilbert closed his copy of the rite and gestured it was time for them all to leave.

Once outside, he motioned to the house and they all went inside. "How long have there been those other voices?" he asked.

"From the beginning, I suppose," said Harry. "That one who said they were leaving . . ." He shook his head with the same look of dismissal he'd shown in the shed. "He always lies. And that other one? Well, you don't want to be listening to him. Stuff he says . . . I was pleased when my wife didn't have to hear it anymore. Put it that way."

Father Gilbert was nodding his understanding though clearly he was more interested in surveying what he was seeing inside the house. "Do you mind, if I look in your lounge?"

Harry led the way and Father Gilbert looked all around.

The statues, holy pictures and religious icons were all pervasive. He walked up to the framed photo of Pope John Paul and nodded approval.

When Father Ward's wound was dressed, they took their leave, undertaking to return the following morning. Harry and Kevin escorted them to the car where Father Gilbert asked Father Ward to drive. The fall on the concrete floor of the shed had bruised his hip and he was in pain. He was grateful when Father Ward agreed and climbed gingerly into the passenger seat. "Home, James," he said cheerfully, "time to lick our wounds and devise a new strategy."

As they motored on out onto the main road, he added, "You did well, Ian."

Unsure in his own mind that was in fact true, Father Ward hesitated before saying, "Thank you."

Father Gilbert laughed. "They will always focus their

attack on the weak link which was deemed to be me on this occasion."

Father Ward drove on in silence for a moment. He was curious and Father Gilbert had given him an opening. "You seemed to falter when the demon quoted that motto: *Malo mori quam foedari*."

"Death before dishonour?"

"Yes."

"You're right, I did. *Malo mori quam foedari* is on my mother's family coat of arms."

"Really?"

"Really."

"How did it know that?"

"I have no idea. We're up against a strong demon. Those other two, they will leave. The weakest always go first, but that violent one will be stubborn. Quoting that motto shows his intention. He wants Mark dead."

"Is it wise to continue?"

Father Gilbert had no quick answer to that.

"Perhaps it's time to alert the medical authorities," said Father Ward, "and have him taken to hospital and placed on a drip to restore his strength."

"Mmmm," replied Father Gilbert, though it was difficult to know if he was agreeing or merely considering the option. "An exorcism is, for want of a better description, a form of torture. You make the unclean spirits so uncomfortable they leave. We seemed to have failed in that regard. That was clear when the two minor demons found their voice."

"Torture," said Father Ward, intrigued now as he was when Father Gilbert had described the rosary in the same terms.

"Yes."

"A spirit does not occupy space or time. Yet they have confined themselves to a, well, for want of a better description, the cramped space of a human body. Leaving seems a good option," said Father Ward.

Father Gilbert smiled. "Mmm," he said, "you'd think so, wouldn't you? But then you'd be misunderstanding the mindset of these spirits. The highest point in God's creation is man. By becoming a man Jesus Christ elevated man even higher. A demon takes possession of a man, becomes incarnate if you will, to degrade that highest point. This demon will not leave easily."

"You think it prudent to continue? If anything happens to Mark . . ."

"I know," Father Gilbert cut him off. "We will pray, Father."

When they arrived home, Father Gilbert went straight to his room to rest. He took off his shoes, lay on the bed covers and was soon in a deep sleep. Despite his best intentions to limit his sleep to an hour, he did not awaken until one o'clock in the morning, when, with what seemed a huge effort, he wearily swung his legs off the bed and sat on the edge, staring off into space, waiting for the fogginess of sleep to lift. He was surprised by the silence in the house and checked his watch. Seeing how much time had elapsed snapped him into greater wakefulness and he went to his sink to splash water on his face.

Knowing he was still very tired and likely to drift off if he stayed in his room to pray, he stole quietly out the back door, took his rosary beads from his pocket and walked up and down the presbytery drive praying. There was a chill in the air and by the time he had finished the rosary he was wide awake and went back inside to kneel at the foot of his bed.

Chapter Sixteen

In the early hours of the morning, when Father Ward went to the toilet, he was aware of activity over at the school and decided to investigate. In the strong light of his torch, he could see a group of boys trying to climb into the school's office window. He walked closer and called out to them. They were shielding their eyes, trying to work out who it was. "You boys better be on your way. The security people are due to call by soon."

It was the priest they realised, and they paused to consider their options. "He's lying," the oldest among them concluded and they ambled off casually into the dark.

Father Ward went back to bed and heard nothing until his alarm sounded the next morning. Finishing his breakfast, he was surprised to see Father Gilbert was not yet up and found him, still kneeling but prone across the counterpane of his bed, gently snoring. He was loath waking him but knew he would want to say Mass before going out to the Alexanders.

Father Gilbert came slowly into the kitchen, his legs stiff and sore. He looked pale and out of sorts. When Father Ward's offer of a cooked breakfast was declined, he regaled Father Gilbert with the story of the intruders while the old priest ate a piece of dry toast and drank a glass of water.

In response to Father Gilbert's recommendation, Harry Alexander came to attend Mass that morning. He arrived late and was clearly upset. After Mass, he waited in the church foyer for them to process out and spoke to them. "Mark tried to set fire to the house last night. Kevin was up and caught him at it. Lots of noise and commotion all night. None of us got a wink of sleep. He still refuses food. I'm thinking we should take him to a hospital."

"We've been thinking the same," said Father Ward and looked to Father Gilbert to take the lead.

"Harry it's entirely up to you," said Father Gilbert. "I can understand your concern."

Harry closed his eyes, took a big breath and walked around in a circle. "I was hoping you could tell me, Father," he said coming back to the priests and looking from one to the other, gripping tightly the brim of his hat.

"Alright then, Harry," said Father Gilbert and indicated the door of the sacristy to avoid those now filing out. Father Ward followed and closed the door.

"Harry," said Father Gilbert, "I'm convinced that whatever's possessed your son will not leave until he is dead. And I don't think hospitalisation will change that. It would be easy to agree with you because if we do proceed we'll be taking a big risk. But, and I have prayed long and hard about this, my intuition tells me, we should proceed."

"Right," said Harry putting on his hat, "that's good enough for me, Father."

"Good," said Father Gilbert, "but we'll need a different strategy. Yesterday, I asked you and your brother to say the rosary during the rite. That didn't happen."

"Sorry, Father."

"I understand. What was happening can be very distracting. But you need to ignore all that."

Harry gave a slight nod, and Father Gilbert could see there was little conviction in the importance of what he had been asked to do.

"As I tried to explain yesterday, saying the rosary is a form of torture. Mary is the complete opposite of what we are up against. She was obedient, a humble servant of God. Satan and those angels who followed him were proud and would not serve. To invoke Mary is like torture to them."

Harry nodded. "I get you, Father. I'll tell Kevin. We'll get that right today."

Father Gilbert undertook to be at the farm within the hour and Harry hurried off. As the priests were about to enter the side door of the garage, they were intercepted by the school principal. "Father Ward," she said quickly, her face a study in anguish, "there's been a break-in at the school. They've taken computers and goodness knows what else."

Father Ward, taking a long moment to recover from this information, eventually said, "You've called the police?"

"Yes. Yes. You didn't hear anything?" she asked.

"Mrs Olsen, Father Gilbert and I really must be going," said Father Ward, avoiding the question. "I'll be in touch."

The principal looked crestfallen and hesitated a moment before reluctantly retreating. "Oh," she said, suddenly remembering and turning back, pointing to the front of the priest's garage, "they've done graffiti all over your garage door."

Father Ward, already disturbed by the news, was at a

loss for words as he tried to make sense of the graffiti, and the principal, seeing she now had his attention, went off vindicated. "I'll see you when you get in touch," she said.

Father Gilbert was amused and chuckled to himself as Father Ward, who had insisted on taking his car, drove out onto the road. Father Ward was not impressed and frowned his disapproval.

"Who would be a parish priest?" asked Father Gilbert and chuckled again. "Off on another fun excursion, with graffiti all over the garage door and a break-in to contend with when we return."

His companion on the journey was at a loss to see how that could in any way be amusing so he explained the sense of irony tickling him. "When I was a young man, I spurned the idea of becoming a diocesan priest. It wasn't tough enough. The diocesan priests I overheard as a boy seemed more interested in rugby, golf and a glass of whiskey over at the presbytery. I held them in contempt. They were worldly. Their talk was not spiritual enough. They fell in too easily with the talk of the laity and, away from the altar, had nothing I saw to define them as men of God. And now here I am in their ranks and finding it almost too hard." He laughed and then broke off into a fit of coughing.

Father Ward glanced across at his passenger. He was worried about Father Gilbert's state of health and told him so. He seemed very low and the wry humour almost a willed rejection of his true state of mind. But the old priest would have none of Father Ward's concern. "When I am weak, I am strong," he said.

This did not impress Father Ward. "I'm just wondering if you might be asking too much of yourself,

Peter," he said.

"Get behind me, Satan," said Father Gilbert, facetiously.

Father Ward did not take offence.

"The cross is hated by Satan," said Father Gilbert, suddenly serious. "You'll remember he tried, through one of the bystanders at the foot of the cross, to persuade Jesus to come down from it. The cross, the rosary, holy water, they are all odious to these unclean spirits. A form of torture. And today," he said, in a forceful and resolved tone, "we will turn up the heat."

"And if we fail?"

"Failure is not an option. We will not fail. This is the work of Jesus. He is Lord of all and these demons will bow to Him."

"I wasn't meaning in that regard, I was meaning fail in terms of preserving the boy's life. I don't need to tell you, Father Gilbert, we live in a world which worships at the shrine of science and believcs everything has a material explanation. Belief in the devil and demons is not in vogue. Exorcisms are considered hocus pocus and as odious to some as burning witches at the stake. If anything happens to this boy, not only will it be a tragedy for the family, but you and I will be pilloried in the media with God knows what consequences to our priesthood."

"Yes," said Father Gilbert.

"Yes?" said Father Ward.

"Yes," repeated Father Gilbert, "and, if you don't mind, I think we would be better served saying the rosary right now. There is no room for fear once you have put your hand to the plough, Father Ward."

Harry and Kevin were waiting for them. They both had rosary beads in hand and were poised to head down to Mark's shed. Their courage and commitment warmed Father Gilbert and he took heart as he approached them.

"Something you ought to know, Father," said Harry, "last night when Kevin and me went down to check on him, before the fire business, Mark was there if you know what I mean."

Father Gilbert nodded.

"As I was leaving, he says to me, 'Help me.' That's all he said. Then that thing was back cursing and carrying on. Wouldn't let the boy eat."

Father Gilbert nodded, "I want to go inside and set things up there."

"In the house," said Harry. "That could be tricky."

"Be that as it may," said Father Gilbert, "bring him to the house please, Harry."

"Right you are," said Harry, "come on Kevin, this'll take the two of us."

Father Ward followed behind down the weed-tufted flagstone path as softly as he could. The rusty hinges of the shed door groaned as Harry pulled it open and ushered the priest into the dark. Father Ward's heart paused a moment then resumed with hard hammer blows against his chest as he waited for light from the drawn curtains to filter into the room.

Mark's eyes bore in on the priest as the two farmers, Harry holding his son's legs and Kevin clasping his chest, lifted Mark off the bed. He writhed and twisted as though host to a giant snake and both men struggled against a feeling of revulsion as they carried him out into the light of day. Up at the house, they sat him in a chair, where he mumbled in a dry, raspy voice, words barely audible. The daylight seemed to change and the atmosphere in the room seemed closer, denser – what Father Ward would later describe as "an awful alteration in the universe, faltering under the weight of a heavy oppression."

Father Gilbert pressed play on a tape-recorder and the room resonated with the sounds of Cistercian monks singing a Gregorian chant. He instructed Father Ward to light coals in a thiruble and burn incense and nodded as the two farmers took their rosary beads from their pockets.

Father Gilbert proceeded. "In the name of Jesus Christ, through the power and authority of his church, I bind you and command you to tell me your name."

Mark was immediately alert, agitated and restless. "*Ire senem*," (Go, old man) snarled the demon, the voice now audible like the hoarse cough of some ancient hag with a peculiar jarring weight to it that resonated like the toll of some funereal bell. Father Gilbert moved in closer and sprinkled Mark with holy water. "In the name of Jesus Christ, tell me your name!"

"My name is Artamal," barked the demon.

"I command you, Artamal, along with your minions now attacking this servant of God, by the mysteries of the incarnation, passion, resurrection and ascension of our Lord Jesus Christ to be gone from this creature of God. I cast you out in the name of our Lord Jesus Christ."

The demons were still.

Father Gilbert held up the cross. "See the cross of the Lord; begone, you hostile powers!"

Suddenly Mark went into convulsions and was

foaming at the mouth.

"I cast you out, Artamal, along with every Satanic power in the name of Our Lord Jesus Christ. Be gone and stay from this creature of God. For it is He who commands you. He who flung you headlong from the heights of heaven into the depths of hell."

The noises from Mark grew louder and louder, a crescendo of howling and babble until he suddenly slumped back into the chair as though the life had gone out of him. The noises were receding, fading into the distance. Harry looked for signs of life. Mark was still breathing and while his father held him in his arms, beneath his lids, his eyes moved, his soul flickering between life and death.

"Mark?"

The eyes slowly opened and a barely discernible change came over him like one utterly exhausted, coming in from traversing a cold and desolate place finding himself safe at home. His consciousness, like a slowly rising tide, came seeping upwards, his eyes came into focus, his shaking hands limply fluttered, the corners of his lips twitched, "Dad."

Harry drew him in closer. He was weeping.

"Mark," said Father Gilbert, "tell me what's happening."

As if unable to speak another word, the boy stared at the priest, panting, and then, summoning a breath, he said, "They've gone," he said, struggling to contain the emotion, until he couldn't and tears flowed down his cheeks. "They've gone," he repeated, looking around the room he had been away from for what seemed a long, long time and reminding himself of all things once so familiar.

Father Gilbert called for the thiruble and, together with Father Ward, sprinkled the home with holy water and incensed every room with the thiruble. "Lord God almighty, bless this home, and under its shelter let there be health, chastity, self-conquest, humility, goodness, mildness, obedience to your commandments, and thanksgiving to God the Father, Son and Holy Spirit. May your blessing remain always in this home and on those who live here through Christ our Lord."

When they were finished they went back to Mark whose father was coaxing him to drink from a glass of water.

Harry moved aside and Father Gilbert drew up a chair alongside his son. "God in his mercy has spared you, Mark."

Mark nodded his agreement.

"Are you ready to renounce the occult and accept Jesus back into your life?"

"I am," said Mark, his voice still hoarse and barely audible.

"Mark," said Father Gilbert, reading from the sacred rite of the church, "do you renounce Satan and all his works?"

"I do," said Mark.

"Do you accept Jesus Christ as your saviour and lord?"

"I do."

Father Gilbert prayed a final blessing and anointed Mark with oil and when he was done Mark attempted to stand, his hand extended. Both priests shook his hand and he thanked them repeatedly. Father Gilbert then asked to speak to Harry in private.

When the two priests returned to Father Ward's car, they found Kevin Alexander loading up the back seat with free range eggs, home kill meat, a box of vegetables and a box of fruit. Father Ward was effuse in his thanks which Kevin waved aside. "Harry's idea not mine, Father. I think he'd give you the title to the farm if you asked him."

"You a Catholic, too, Kevin?" asked Father Gilbert.

"Yes," said Kevin, a little abashed by the admission.

"Haven't seen you at Mass."

"No. But that's about to change. I thought church was just for the women folk. But I see the power and strength in it now. What you fellahs did in there. . ." He took a big breath and blew it out. "Full marks to yuhs and thank God there's priests is all I can say."

Immediately, they were beyond the farm gate, Father Ward's first comment was, "That was so quick."

"Mmmm, my word yes," said Father Gilbert. "But I've seen quicker. First exorcism I ever assisted took less than a minute. I was with the former diocesan exorcist and all he had to do was mention the name of Jesus and it was all over. But every one of them is different. That one needed fasting and prayer."

"And the full range of all things demons hate."

"Exactly," agreed Father Gilbert and the two priests drove on in silence, enjoying an immense sense of relief and satisfaction that brooked no words.

As they were about to pull onto the main road another vehicle approached, the driver, a woman, coming from the opposite direction had recognised Father Ward's vehicle and was tooting insistently to catch his attention. As the driver drew closer, they recognised her as Mrs Alexander. She skidded to a stop and rushed from her car. Father Ward wound down his window and drew back as she flung herself up against the door and reached in to take hold of him.

Realising, from the joyous look on her face, the move was probably benign, he leaned back towards her and she grabbed him in a hug. She was crying and laughing at the same time and kept saying thank you. When she caught her breath and stood back, she explained Harry had called with the good news and then, aware of her omission, she hurried quickly around to Father Gilbert's side of the car. She was not as confident in her approach to the other priest and Father Gilbert, in an effort to reassure her, climbed out to greet her.

"Oh, Father Gilbert," she said and, too choked with emotion to continue, she turned aside, with her head in her hands and wept. Composing herself, she came back to the priest. "Oh, Father Gilbert, I'm so sorry."

"No, no, no," said Father Gilbert gently placing his hand on her shoulder.

"Oh, but I am. I should never have listened to Jenny Walters. You're such a good priest. I'm so sorry. I'm so sorry. I'm so sorry." All this between convulsions of tears.

"Do I get a hug?" interrupted Father Gilbert.

Mrs Alexander laughed and swung her arms around the old priest in a fierce, long embrace. "I'm sorry too for what you've been through with our Mark," she said, stepping back and wiping her eyes.

"All in a day's work. Happy to help."

Mrs Alexander was distracted by all the produce in the back seat of the car. "Those men haven't given you any of my preserves or my jams."

"Oh," said Father Gilbert, "they've been more than

generous."

"I'll bring some in tomorrow," she said.

Another car had turned into the road and wanted to get past, forcing Mrs Alexander to break off her effusive outpouring of thanks.

Father Gilbert had one more thing to say. "I spoke to Harry, asked him to pass on a message. Mark has definitely accepted God back into his life, but he needs to find God in his own way. It won't be your way."

"Father, don't you worry about that. I've had time to think. I know where I went wrong. Don't you worry about that."

When she arrived home, the three men were in the lounge watching cricket on the television. Her quiet entry was not noticed and she stood unobserved watching them, watching Mark until they felt her eyes upon them and turned off the television. Both mother and son were tentative in their approach to one another.

Mrs Alexander could see all her husband had reported was true and Mark was tender in his greeting. "Mum," he said.

"Oh," she said, unable to hold back another moment and took him in a warm embrace that seemed to go on and on, until she broke off and stood back to take him in. "You need fattening up," she said and was soon full of business preparing his favourite meal.

After the meal and after Kevin had gone, in a bid to please his wife and in keeping with her habit of always saying the rosary in the lounge after dinner, Harry asked if she would like to. "No, no," she said "let's watch the cricket."

"You sure?"

"Of course I'm sure. I can say the rosary in my room later."

Chapter Seventeen

Father Ward and Father Gilbert had planned on a celebration the following Tuesday before Father Gilbert left the parish. He had reluctantly agreed to accompany Father Ward on a tramp, a very short hike, he was assured by the young priest, through native bush to a nearby lake. "Even an elderly, lame priest can do it with ease, Peter," was Father Ward's pledge and they had planned to leave after saying midday Mass for the school children. But, as Death would have it, Father Ward received an urgent call from the hospital. An old man was dying and his family was requesting a priest.

It was not a quick visit and Father Ward had to manoeuvre his way through a minefield of opposing views on the Catholic Church and the sacraments which halted proceedings for a long time. Half of the dying man's relations wanted him to administer the last rites and the other half were very vocal in their opposition. The dying man didn't seem in a position to express his view on the matter either way, and, because he was not someone Father Ward had ever seen at Mass, he too, wondered about the appropriateness of giving him the last sacrament. In the end, someone claimed they saw the heavily medicated man give a slight nod of his head and that carried the day. Father Ward administered extreme unction.

He arrived back in the middle of the afternoon. The picnic hamper was still there on the kitchen table and Father Gilbert was dozing in the lounge, with Mozart playing in the background. He had not changed out of his hiking clothes and sat upright when Father Ward entered the room.

"That has to have been the longest last rites on record," said Father Gilbert, impishly.

Father Ward gave a derisive snort and slumped in a chair. "There was a lot of talking to do and when I finally gave him the sacrament I had to wonder if there was any benefit in it. The man was full of opiates and gave the impression he was hallucinating. He certainly wasn't looking at me. Had his eyes wide open looking past me at something. When he stopped staring at whatever it was, his eyes went all around the room taking everyone and everything in, as though he knew it was for the last time. He seemed lost and afraid and I'm not sure anything I said registered."

"People on the sidelines of death are doomed to be clumsy despite the best of intentions," said Father Gilbert.

"I think I could've done better."

"Mmm," said Father Gilbert standing, "Be that as it may, we have a hike to go on."

Father Ward closed his eyes.

"Come on, Ian, you've sold the idea to me. Now, let's get to that lake before nightfall."

By the time they arrived at the entrance to the bush, the light was failing and Father Gilbert's slow passage along the uneven path made Father Ward wonder if they would even get to see the lake. Father Gilbert was more buoyant. "The tender gloom and the wan light," he said, quoting from some obscure poem.

They arrived at twilight, with birds silhouetted against a purple and red sky, as they flew back in for the night to the bush surrounding the lake. The noise of their return disturbed the peace of the place, but not the beauty. The light of the moon was already upon the serene waters reflecting the flight of the birds and the changing colours of a darkening sky.

The priests gathered firewood, lit a small fire near the lake's edge and Father Gilbert took out his old coffee pot to prop in the embers when the fire died down. Father Ward had set up the two old canvas deck chairs Father Gilbert had insisted on bringing. The hamper was packed with chicken legs and salad and sandwiches and they sat in comfort and ate hearty as the cacophony of the birds faded and left them in silence.

"Oh," said Father Ward suddenly remembering something, "I had a curious encounter the other day. We were tramping over one of the big Maori stations and Brad Rameka came by on his horse. He's a shepherd. That big man who came to the presbytery to say he had re-enrolled his daughter at the school. He stands in the foyer at Mass."

"Oh, yes," said Father Gilbert.

"He told me he'd heard a fellow saying bad things about you at the pub."

"Dean?" said Father Gilbert.

"I think so. Anyway, he told me to tell you that he wouldn't be doing it anymore."

"I see," said Father Gilbert. "Poor Dean."

"Yes, poor Dean. Someone else at the pub said Brad beat the by joves out of him. Very protective of priests are the Ramekas, it seems."

"Especially after one of them comes around for a kai and looks out for their daughter," said Father Gilbert, smiling.

The sky was ablaze with stars and there was a gentle breeze coming off the lake shifting the flames of the fire as Father Gilbert found some embers to place his coffee pot on. The scuffling of some small creature in the nearby bush came in on the quiet.

Father Ward waited until Father Gilbert's coffee was ready before opening his bottle of wine and proposing a toast. "To you, Peter, a good priest, a good exorcist and a good friend." He clinked his glass into Father Gilbert's coffee cup. They drank and Father Gilbert called for a recharge and held his coffee cup up again. "And here's to you, Ian. A good priest. Brave and true."

Father Ward was genuinely touched by this, and, in the years to come, during periods of doubt, he recalled them like some mantra that lifted his spirits. He had grown fond of this old priest and his eccentric ways; and he held out the hope he might stay on. But, when Father Gilbert submitted his report to the bishop, he was summoned back to Auckland, to the retirement home and did not challenge the recall. He was tired and he needed to rest. "Age with his stealing steps," he said, quoting the bard, "Hath clawed me in his clutch." His imminent departure saddened the occasion and they both felt it.

The crackle of the fire as it all burned down to embers and the hush of the evening was soothing and neither man spoke as they reflected on their time together, something each knew the other was doing, without having to say it.

Taken in retrospect, as a chain of events, one on top of the other, the memory seemed like something from an overworked narrative, too much for any man's patience and tolerance. "Who would be a priest eh, Peter?" asked Father Ward, suddenly coming in on the silence.

"Not many these days, Ian. If it wasn't for the Filipino priests coming here, we'd be in trouble."

"One of the family of that dying man I was called out to today escorted me to my car, after I had given the old man the last rites. A young man he was, and he, like me, had been witness to all the bickering and arguing of his family, after I arrived and he commiserated. 'Hard being a priest eh, Father?' he said to me and I said nothing. But I've been thinking about that and asking myself the question, why do I keep going?"

"Probably the least preferred occupation in the country," said Father Gilbert. "The media have seen to that."

"I know and everyone's view of the priesthood has been tainted." And that was as much as Father Ward wanted to say on that subject and as much as his fellow priest wanted to hear. He sipped his wine and went on, "Sitting out here in this wonderfully comfortable concession to civilization," he said, nestling back into the folds of his chair, "I have an answer to my own question." He looked up at the stars and breathed in on the freshening night air. "And it's this: when I'm vesting for Mass of a Sunday morning and I see through the sacristy window my parishioners filing into the church: the old, the young, the families, that good, faithful remnant of Catholics who keep coming every Sunday, I am reminded of their depth, their holiness, their sincerity, their immense generosity and I'm pleased I'm a priest.

"And when I stand at the altar and consecrate the bread and wine into the precious body, blood, soul and divinity of Our Blessed Lord, the creator of all this," he said and threw his hands up to the sky, "and I look out on that sea of faces watching every move I make, intent and expectant, I'm pleased I'm a priest.

"But more than any of that . . . More than any of that . . . When I sit down after distributing holy communion, during that time of silent prayer, when heart speaks to heart and I feel His presence, His peace, His love and His mercy and I look out on the congregation and know they are feeling the same because God has come to visit His people and He is making His presence known in the silence of their hearts, that peaceful, reassuring presence that brings them back week after week. And I know they are going to leave the church different to when they arrived, that they have been strengthened for what the week ahead brings because they carry with them the King of Kings, I'm pleased to be a priest because only a priest can give that."

Father Gilbert did what he often did: he said nothing. But he was nodding thoughtfully, and Father Ward could see the hint of a smile in the firelight.

"And you?" asked Father Ward.

"All of that," he said. "All of that."

The two priests fell silent, and Father Gilbert shifted his coffee pot to the centre of the dying fire. He waited until the coffee was boiling and went to pick up the pot to fill his cup but thought better of it and put the cup down on the ground. He went to speak and stopped himself and let out a long breath. "Can you imagine, Ian, knowing all you have just described what it was to be me and the burden I carry. A consecrated priest drunk and asleep under Grafton Bridge. A consecrated priest lying with a woman. A consecrated priest fathering a child. The shame of it was more than I could bear, and no amount of alcohol could block it out. Because you see, I never lost belief in God. But what I never really believed was: He never lost His belief in me, either. But it was true. Can you imagine what it was like to believe He actually wanted *me* back as a priest?"

Father Ward frowned at Father Gilbert's earnest look. "No," he finally said.

"Fair enough," said Father Gilbert. "Not something I hope you ever have to experience." He smiled. "My mother was obviously guided in christening me Peter, only I had let the Lord down so much more than my namesake. And yet, He kept after me.

"Imagine this if you will, a fallen priest like me not only given another chance but then asked to be an exorcist? The devil had had his way with me. I had shown myself to be weak and easily defeated, and yet the bishop was asking me to stand up to him, to deliver others from him. The irony of it still amuses me.

"But you ask me why I'm a priest and here I stand with you and all you have said about the privilege of being able to offer His people the Eucharist, but I also add to that something else: all I have experienced over the years as the diocesan exorcist.

"When I go up against Satan and his demons, I have nothing of my own to offer. All I have is Jesus Christ. And that man from Galilee, God incarnate, always comes to my aid. He is always there for me." Father Gilbert faltered and took a moment to collect himself. "He is always there for me. I stand before the prince of darkness, before evil beyond all imaginings, before the prompter of all unutterable atrocities of man against man and I have nothing in and of myself to defeat him. Nothing. And the Lord of all lords, the one in whom all things have their being is there for me, with love beyond anything I could ask for or imagine. And that's when I know I'm glad I'm a priest. I'm glad I've answered His call. He has given me a second chance to do what only a priest can do for His people."

Glossary of Catholic terms

Act of contrition: *a prayer seeking God's forgiveness for sins committed.*

Aspergillium: *an implement for sprinkling holy water.*

Columban missionaries: *Catholic missionary society founded in Ireland in 1917 with Saint Columban as its patron saint.*

Crucifix: *a cross with the figure of Christ as distinct from a bare cross.*

Guardian angel: *an angel assigned by God to protect a person from evil.*

Morning offering: *A morning prayer offering the prayers, works and sufferings of the day to God.*

Persona Christi: *in the person of Christ.*

Prie-dieu: *a piece of furniture for use during prayer, consisting of a kneeling surface and a narrow upright front to rest the elbows and place books.*

Tabernacle: *a receptacle for the consecrated element of the Eucharist.*

Traditional Catholic: *a Catholic who subscribes to the pre-Vatican II Latin tradition of Catholicism.*

Scapula: *an object of piety designed to show the wearer's pledge to a saint or way of life.*

Stole: *a liturgical vestment, a band of coloured clothe, about six feet long, three inches wide and worn around the neck.*

ABOUT THE AUTHOR

Mark Chamberlain is an award-winning author.
His work has featured on Radio New Zealand.

Mark's writing presentations for teachers have featured in conferences both in Europe (ECIS) and the Middle East (TARA and NESA). He has presented as an author in international schools in the Middle East and schools in New Zealand (LNNZ) and Australia.

He has worked as a truck driver, a fisherman, a dishwasher, a probation officer, a drain digger, a factory worker, a pokie machine attendant, a scrub cutter, a drug and alcohol abuse counsellor and one night as a bouncer. Since marrying Eleanor and settling down, most of his jobs have been in teaching or journalism and other forms of writing. He lives hidden away in the Far North of New Zealand and divides his time between fishing, hunting, planting trees and spraying for gorse and kikuyu, with writing thrown in on the side during the winter months.

ALSO, BY M. O. CHAMBERLAIN

HISTORICAL FICTION
Lawrence of Arabia: Desert Wolf
Whenua
Whenua II

SHORT STORY COLLECTION
The Collector for the IRA and other Short Stories

TEACHER MANUALS
Releasing Reluctant Writers
Best of the Best

BIOGRAPHY
With a Father Like Mine

FICTION
Harry's Road trip to Valhalla
Dangerous
Dangerous II
Pure
Mammon

COMEDY
Gerald and Lucille

NONFICTION
NZ Immigrants: Their Stories

Made in the USA
Columbia, SC
02 July 2022

62578216R00112